KING OF
FLAMES

BOOKS BY KATHRYN ANN KINGSLEY

THE MASKS OF UNDER SERIES

King of Shadows

Queen of Dreams

THE IRON CRYSTAL SERIES

To Charm a Dark Prince

To Bind a Dark Heart

To Break a Dark Cage

To Love a Dark Lord

For a full list, visit www.kathrynkingsley.com

KATHRYN ANN
KINGSLEY

KING OF
FLAMES

SECOND SKY

Published by Second Sky in 2024

An imprint of Storyfire Ltd.
Carmelite House
50 Victoria Embankment
London EC4Y 0DZ
United Kingdom

www.secondskybooks.com

ONE

For in that sleep of death what dreams may come?

How utterly fascinating.

Aon was quite accustomed to dreaming. Especially in this state, trapped as he was between waking and not, as he waited out the years in his crypt. But they were always memories. Never anything new. Never anything *real*.

This was not a memory.

He was standing in a bedroom. It was small with heavy curtains drawn over the windows to blot out the dim light of the early dawn. He could hear the muffled rumble of machinery and human life. But it was not the bedroom itself that had captured his attention.

No, it was the figure of the young woman asleep in the mundane bed.

Aon sat down on the edge of her mattress, reaching his hand out to touch her cheek. Why he did it, he could not say. For all his thousand years of life, he had never experienced anything quite like this moment.

He rested the tips of the talons of his clawed, metal hand on her cheek. She did not stir. But neither did his touch pass through her as though she, or he, were a phantasm. Curling his finger in toward his palm, he brushed a strand of her blonde hair away from her face to better study her features.

A beautiful young thing. Free of the worries of mortal life in her sleep, her skin was smooth in her repose. Curious. Who was she? How could she have called him here? Was she some kind of magus? No... she did not seem to have the ability to summon him. Certainly not subconsciously. Then, why? And how?

"What do we have here?"

She shifted at the sound of his voice, rolling onto her back. She was wearing only a thin slip for a top, her skin illuminated by the electric light obscured by the curtains over her windows. It was then, that he saw it. The mark upon her forearm, written in the language of his people. He smiled beneath the full metal mask that obscured his face. Ah... well. How *wonderful.*

Leaning down over her, he whispered to the sleeping young woman. "I will see you soon, little one... and what fun we shall have."

* * *

"Get off, get off, *get off!*"

Turns out that shouting at a tattoo wasn't very effective, go figure. To be fair, Lydia hadn't expected it to work. It probably would have been worse if it had. But seeing as she hadn't gone to bed with the weird mark on her forearm, all bets were admittedly off.

Sighing, she chucked the Brillo pad she had been attacking herself with into the sink and looked down at the thing on her arm. The skin was red and raw from the myriad of cleaners—Hell, she'd even tried straight bleach—but nothing she'd done had even gotten it to smudge.

Like it was a tattoo. A real tattoo. That she really, *really* shouldn't have. When she'd woken up and saw it while making herself coffee, it had looked like it had been there for ages. Which only made her more confused.

How had it shown up? What was it? *Why* was it there?

It looked like any old tattoo. It was small, about the size of a nickel, and done as if in a single pass with black ink from a needle. It was just a single symbol—archaic, strange, and nothing she recognized. It was in the shape of a backward N with a spiral cut through the middle.

Rubbing her hands over her face, she let out a defeated sigh. She'd call out sick from work to go to the doctors over it—but what would they even say? *Don't get so drunk.* She hadn't been. *Drugs?* No. *A prank?* The doors and windows were all locked when she woke up.

No, there was nothing a doctor could do. They'd probably just refer her to a psychiatrist. Or a psych ward.

Besides, she was all out of sick days. She had to go in, otherwise she'd get her pay docked. And in Boston, she could barely afford her one-bedroom apartment as it was. She liked having a bank account. So off she went to the T, bundled up against the dreary November weather. It was the Wednesday before Thanksgiving, and nobody was happy to be there. Herself, included. But she had a job to do, so she joined the groggy masses on the early morning commute.

With a thing on her arm.

That shouldn't be there.

That really fucking itched now.

Though, that bit wasn't the tattoo's fault. That was entirely the bleach, scrubbing pads, and panicked nail-scratching she'd done at it in a desperate attempt to get it off. She pulled out her phone and started searching for everything she possibly could that might lead her to a diagnosis for whatever the thing was.

Shocker, *WebMD* didn't have anything for "surprise tattoo."

Whatever.

Her phone buzzed with a text message from Nick, her best friend from college who worked as a security guard for her building. They'd been interns at the medical center together, way back when. But where she'd wound up... *kind of* in a medical setting, Nick had a penchant for not trying very hard unless he was really interested. Very little interested him, and so security was the perfect spot for him.

u in today?

Man, she really wished he'd used full sentences. She sent back:

Yeah, running a little late. Think my clients will be pissed?

Nick replied with a skull and crossbones emoji. She huffed a laugh. It was a bit of a running gag between them. A second later, he added:

No more than usual.

Her clients wouldn't be pissed. Her clients wouldn't be anything, actually. Nothing against them—they couldn't help it.

They were dead, after all.

Lydia was a forensic autopsy technician. With every person she ever met, she had to explain why her job was not like that thing they saw on *CSI* that one time. It was hardly that interesting. Her job was only to collect the data. Record the numbers.

There were more important, better-paid, smarter people who sat at a desk and solved the crimes. She just stuck plastic sticks in dead people, cut bits and pieces out of them for various reasons, and took a whole lot of gross photos.

Contrary to popular belief, nobody worked the night shift at a morgue, even if horror movies told you otherwise. She had a normal, nine-to-five, humdrum life, just like most people.

Even if hers had to do with dead people.

Well, hey, somebody had to do it.

It did sometimes leave her with the scent of chemicals, though. She had to use mint shampoo because if she used anything floral, she just came off smelling like a funeral parlor.

Leaning against the side of the train car, she looked down at her phone and flicked her thumb to scroll through the list of web links in search of anything, anywhere, that referenced mystery tattoos.

The subway car slowed to a stop. As they were nowhere near a station, that meant the green line was backed up. Again.

It was funny that in the city of Boston, you could hit the start of your workday by fifteen minutes in either direction, and honestly, nobody cared. Boston's T was America's oldest subway station, and it showed. At this point, she suspected if a pigeon shat on the rails, the train would have to wait twenty minutes for it to dry.

She didn't even want to think about what happened when it snowed.

Lydia kept scratching her arm over her sleeve. The heavy chemicals she used on her surprise tattoo were itching like mad. Maybe she shouldn't have attacked it with a Brillo pad and bleach, but she had been frantic. Rolling up her sleeve, she tried to surreptitiously glance at it to see if it had magically disappeared. Maybe the bleach had done its trick. But no. There, surrounded by a red rash of her own doing, was the mark.

It didn't even hurt like she had expected a new tattoo probably should. It hadn't felt like anything until she attacked it trying to get it off. It was like it had been there for years.

She bounced her leg nervously for a moment as she took a

deep breath before letting it out. There wasn't a point in panicking. No point at all.

Lydia wasn't the type to cry and panic. She considered herself a rational, reasonable, logical human being. In college and med school, she had worked as an entry-level EMT. She had learned the "act first, panic later" mantra from a few of the older, far more beautifully jaded and saltier Boston paramedics.

They were a particular bunch.

The method was clear—solve the problem, then have a breakdown if you had to.

Act first, panic later. Act first, panic later.

All the way to work, she scratched absentmindedly at the spot on her arm. Passing the front desk, she threw her bag onto the track of the X-ray machine.

Government building, government security. It was the office of the Chief Medical Examiner, after all, and it wasn't exactly in the nicest part of town. Even if it was attached to the Boston Medical Center, it was a few blocks from the corrections center and, in that, no man's land between the South End and I-93 where it came back out of the Big Dig. It was probably the only *seriously* sketchy part of Boston.

All sorts of people tried to wander in, some high, some nuts, most somewhere in between.

"There you are," Nick greeted her from behind the security booth glass. He scratched at the collar of his shirt. "Thought you'd never show up." He didn't look up from his tablet.

"Yeah, yeah. Rough morning."

"The sexy kind?" He grinned at her. He had an endearing, lopsided smile and scruffy brown hair. She figured he spent as little time as possible combing it without looking like a complete hobo. He was the kind of guy who always wore a T-shirt, over which he always wore either a hoodie or his uniform. That was pretty much all she'd ever seen him wear.

"Nope. Just the boring kind." She didn't mention the tattoo. She didn't even know how to bring it up.

"Beer? Tonight?"

"Sure," Lydia agreed to after-work beers without really thinking about it. "Why not?" Screw it. She could use a drink. Maybe she could show Nick the mark on her arm, and he might —*might*—not think she was crazy.

"Cool," he said and went back to his tablet, dismissing her from the conversation. Oh, Nick and his stellar lack of people skills.

Lydia picked up her bag from the other side of the X-ray machine. Nick hadn't even bothered to look at the screen; he never did. Shouldering the bag, she headed toward her area of the lab. She had a desk, a few trays for bodies—the typical setup. She wasn't a manager, she wasn't particularly senior, she just sort of... existed, and did her job. And that seemed fine by everybody, including her.

Flopping down at her desk, Lydia realized there was a body on her metal table. It was still in its bag, likely having just been dropped off. Lydia blinked. There wasn't one scheduled for today. A folder on her desk had a sticky note on it, saying in fine-point Sharpie scrawl:

You're the lucky winner. –Jim.

Jim was her boss. He was funny, they had a friendly and casual working relationship, and he trusted her to get her job done. Even better, he didn't over-manage her, and in exchange, she didn't ask him for a damn thing except for time off. Lydia was as self-reliant as employees came and managed her own time without an issue. It was a pleasant, peaceful coexistence.

But it also meant when he needed to get something done and done fast, it was her job.

Sighing, Lydia picked up the folder and opened it. The

body would have been in the fridge, except Jim had pulled it specifically. She scanned the first few lines of text and groaned. This was going to be an obnoxious one.

The gentle term they used on the form was "unexpected." Lydia, with her off-color sense of humor, had long since dubbed it "murdery."

There were a few different kinds of people who worked in the dead-people business. There were those who had simply turned that part of them off and handled everything they saw and did like a bank clerk. No big deal, nothing to see here, move right along. There were those who internalized it to the point they became dead inside themselves. And then there were ones like her, who handled it with humor. It was a crass and morbid way of dealing with the world, but at least it was good for a laugh.

Better that than winding up like that guy from *Phantasm*. What was his name again? The Tall Man. Right. It'd been a while since she'd seen that one, and if she could recall right, he'd been some weird brain-sucking alien or something. She didn't remember, except that he had those bizarre floating silver orbs.

Lydia loved horror movies. From the age of eight and on, her dad would take her to the local Blockbuster every Friday, where she could rent two VHS tapes. So she did, and every week, they were always from the horror section. Lydia had spent her childhood working alphabetically through from *13 Ghosts* all the way down to *Wolfman*.

None of it had ever really scared her. As a kid, all she'd ever wonder about the movies was whether Michael Myers ever got lonely, or how Pinhead slept at night with all those things in his face. Did he have to straighten them all back out in the morning with the back of a hammer?

It was part of her love of horror that led her to do what she did for a living. It was easier to handle, in some weird way, if you just pretended it was all movie magic. These weren't real squishy people—they were just props.

She refocused on the folder for the dead guy on the slab, and flipped over to the police report. The guy had been found the night prior in an alley between some buildings in Boylston. All that was scribbled down was that the man had died from an apparent shotgun wound to the chest. No other descriptions, no other boxes checked. Even the little box that indicated if a weapon was found nearby was left blank. Freaking cops. They never wrote down anything that mattered. More than once, she had wound up doing a cast of a blade only to be told another department had the knife the whole time.

With a sigh, Lydia stood and walked up to the body. Putting on a sterile hair cap, she suited up and threw on a pair of gloves from the table next to it and unzipped the bag. She pulled it all the way down past the toes before opening it up.

"Well, hey there, fancy buddy," Lydia greeted the dead body incredulously and tilted her head to the side. That was something you didn't see every day. The man was dressed in what looked like Victorian clothes. Shirt, vest, and coat, all extremely dated and all in shades of white and cream. Even his shoes were white and polished. Was this guy on the way to a wedding? Or a costume ball, maybe?

Blood had oozed from his forehead and ran straight down toward his chin, revealing it had been there while the man was standing. It covered the right side of his face, obscuring what would have been otherwise reasonably handsome features. He had short black hair, the only thing about him that wasn't white, cream, or in the case of his skin, the familiar lifeless pale blue of a corpse.

"Signs of an altercation before death," Lydia mumbled to herself as she wrote it down on her notebook. That would be the only reason he had blood streaking down his face like that. What had killed the man was pretty clear—a broad swath of small holes in his chest, each circled and ringed in dried blood. A shotgun blast to the chest, and it looked like it was done from close range and been packed with buckshot. Great. *Who the fuck packs buckshot in Boston?* Probably a homeless guy hunting raccoons, honestly.

She found herself deeply annoyed at the murderer. Buckshot would make for some serious fun all afternoon as she picked each individual ball out of his chest. So much for a short day before Thanksgiving.

The man had no identification on him at the scene. In fact, his pockets had been entirely emptied. That wasn't uncommon, even if most people didn't generally get mugged with a shotgun on the way to a costume ball. Lydia had to admit at least that part made it interesting.

First step, photos, then strip a layer of bizarre Victorian clothing, and more snaps with her camera. The clothes weren't cheap and didn't seem like they were costumes. Once the body was naked, she took more pictures, bagged and tagged the clothes, and put them in a little plastic bin on the bottom shelf for the more traditional forensic teams to examine.

The lab would want a blood sample. They always did, no matter how obvious the cause of death might be. Drugs, blah, blah, blah. Lydia took a red washable pen, circled a mark on his femoral artery on this thigh, and inserted a syringe. He'd only been dead twelve to fourteen hours, as far as she could tell, so it'd be easy to get a blood test. When she pulled back the plunger, it was dry. Just air.

What...?

She threw the needle into the hazmat bin by her feet and picked up another one, and this time, circled a different spot on the femoral artery. Lydia drew back the plunger and... nope. Nothing. No blood.

The hell?

Okay, the subclavian, then. No blood. All right. Screw it.

Screw this guy. Going to a stack of drawers, she rummaged through a bin and found a cardiac stick. Go for the gold. She unwrapped it, went to the body, and fed it into his heart.

Nothing.

Okay! Okay, fine. He had no blood in his body. Completely exsanguinated. Sure, why the hell not. She took off her gloves and started to write notes on one of her forms, detailing what she'd found, or, in this case, not found.

Lydia could start doing a cut-down and pull open the guy's ribcage to see if he was utterly devoid of blood, but that was a hell of a lot of work to do without being explicitly told to do it. The corpse hadn't started decomp yet, so he hadn't been dead long enough that the blood would have pooled into the tissue. The man didn't have bullet wounds large enough to have bled him out. Where did all the blood go?

Whatever. Let someone further up the food chain solve the mystery.

Lydia took a few more photos of the shotgun wounds on his chest before taking a swab and beginning to clean each one. It seemed that the only blood this guy had was the dry stuff on the outside of his body. Oh, well.

Picking up a small pile of little red sticks, she began to feed each one into the bullet wounds. It always reminded her of playing *KerPlunk*. Taking a photo, she wrote that the weapon was likely operated by someone standing between three to five feet away and at chest level. Pulling all the red sticks back out and dropping them into the hazmat bin, it was time to stop avoiding the inevitable.

Picking up a pair of thin, needle-nose tweezers, she began plucking out the little balls of lead, one by one.

Tink.

A little lead ball went into the tray. At least the wounds weren't too deep. A few inches at most. Enough to kill and wind up in the lungs and the heart, but not enough that she had to really go digging.

Tink.

So much for a peaceful last day before Thanksgiving break. She was going to be at this for way too long. It had already been forty-five minutes, and Lydia was barely halfway through.

Tink.

Each time she pulled out a ball, she marked the wound with a tiny red dot of her washable pen. That way, she wouldn't have to play the guessing game of which ones she had already done. That was the worst.

Tink.

The mindless, repetitive task let her mind wander. Of course, naturally, it strayed right back to dwelling about the mark on her arm. What the hell was it? How the hell did it get there? What kind of sick joke was this? How could she get the stupid mark off her forearm?

Tink.

At least she was almost done with the buckshot. Just a few more little pieces of lead to go. That last one had been deeper than the others.

Tink.

Lydia nearly jumped a foot in the air as her desk phone rang. With a sigh, she put down the tweezers, pulled off her goggles and gloves, and went to answer it. "Yeah?"

"Hey, Lydia," answered her boss, Jim. "Wondering if you could take a mugshot of our dapper John Doe. Upstairs wants to circulate a description before they leave for the day."

"It's not even two in the afternoon."

"Holiday."

Lydia shook her head. Must be nice. Of course, the fucking suits upstairs got to leave early while she sat there playing *Operation.* "Yeah, sure, I'm on it."

"You're the best. Oh, and don't forget a dental impression for ID," Jim replied, and she heard the click as he hung up.

Lydia put the phone down and slid on yet another pair of clean gloves. "All right, Dapper John." She had to give Jim some credit for the fitting nickname. "Time to smile for the camera."

Taking a few more shots of his face with the blood smear, she then set to work cleaning the dry, congealed substance from his features to get a clean shot. It was when she went to get some of the blood off his temple that she paused. It looked like something else was there, under the blood.

This guy was just full of surprises.

Tossing the bloody swab into the hazmat, she picked up another to scrub at that spot further. It looked like there was some kind of white ink on his face. Two marks looked as though they were tattooed on him. White tattoos were rare, especially on the face. A gang member, maybe? Once she had cleaned the rest of the blood off, she turned his head to the side, stiff but still flexible, to get a better look at the marks.

Lydia pulled back, her eyes wide.

They matched the symbol on her arm. Her "surprise tattoo." His marks weren't exactly the same—no backward N with a spiral—but the bizarre, archaic, pointed style was unmistakable. Like different characters from the same alphabet.

Wide-eyed and dumbfounded, Lydia froze. How was this possible? Lydia's heart was pounding in her ears as she tried to make sense of what she was seeing. All at once she was thinking too quickly and not fast enough, her thoughts a jumbled mess as they tried to vie for supremacy.

Nothing had a chance to win the fight and rise to the surface. No matter how weird her day had started, it was about to get much, *much* much worse.

A hand snapped around her wrist. Cold, deathly, and wrong. The face of the corpse turned to look at her of its own accord. Eyes, dilated and ringed in red, met hers.

Lydia screamed.

TWO

Tattoos didn't just appear overnight.

A dead body didn't just sit up.

Being a proud connoisseur of all things horror, Lydia had believed that should a scenario like the ones on the screen ever come true, she would simply scoop up the nearest weapon and dispatch the monster without much fuss. How many times had she ridiculed the busty actress for doing something stupid? For crying and panicking and fleeing upstairs when, really, they should simply accept the monster's existence and do what needed to be done to survive?

Well, here she was. This was her moment.

This was the bit she had daydreamed about since she was a kid. It turned out it was a lot easier to scoff when you weren't the one sitting on the VCT, looking up at a toothy and angry monster trying to kill you.

When you're sitting on your sofa, it's easy to judge.

So, what would she do when faced with a monster? This daydream-gone-nightmare, turned to life, sitting on the table with hungry red eyes boring into her as a crocodile looks at his lunch?

Surely, she'd defend herself. Grab the mallet labeled "for hard cases only" from the bin and crack its skull open. Or grab a scalpel. Or anything. It always looked so simple in the movies.

Turns out—nope.

Not so much.

Lydia just sat there agog, her brain skipping like a needle on a record. This couldn't be real. This couldn't be happening. Somewhere in the back of her mind, behind all the fear and the instant rush of adrenaline, she apologized to the fictional characters for having thought she was somehow superior.

The man was just as pale as he had been moments before. The same lifeless, cold, white and veiny blue-ish tone that dead bodies took on some half dozen hours after their deaths. But instead of the passive, stoic face of a corpse, its features were twisted in rage. In *hunger.*

It was going to eat her.

"Holy shit—" was all Lydia finally managed to summon as she half sat, half lay on the floor, looking up at an impossible monster. No blood was oozing from the holes in his chest.

The creature on the table was fixed on her with crimson eyes. The corpse grinned an expression that promised nothing but pain. His canines were long—too long. They protruded against his lower lip as he seemed to sincerely enjoy the thought of whatever he was planning to do to her.

Fuck.

Lydia had seen enough horror movies to know what he was. She wasn't even going to say the word to herself. No way in hell was she going to dignify the ridiculous situation she was in by naming the thing that was in front of her.

Luckily, the newly-awoken-monster-corpse didn't quite have his legs under him yet. His hungry, fierce hiss in Lydia's direction had been followed by a rather unceremonious collapse onto the concrete floor with a hard crack. Lydia did her best to finally scramble up to her feet and nearly took another table down with her in the process.

Its haze didn't seem to deter it much. It was crawling after Lydia on the ground, snarling and growling, pale and translucent lips pulled back from the too-long white teeth. That was all it took for her to declare "nope" and decide self-defense was not an option. Lydia somehow had the presence of mind to snatch up her phone as she ran by the desk on the way to the door out of her office.

"Get back here!" an angry voice shouted. It sounded raspy and dry like he had swallowed rocks.

The corpse could talk.

Why not.

There was a roar and a hissing sound from behind her. As she slammed the door shut, she whirled, unable to resist the temptation to look at the creature that had once been a corpse on her slab. The monster, uncaring for his nudity, was standing now and lurching toward the door, his face still twisted in rage.

Adrenaline pounded through her body, and she took off running down the hallway as it crashed into the door. She didn't look back again to see what was happening. She knew the creature was going to chase her.

"Do not run!" the monster snarled.

"Help!" she screamed as she tore ass down the tile-walled hallway, looking for somebody—anybody. "Somebody, *help!*"

She rounded the corner toward the fire exit and felt her heart leap into her throat at what she saw. Skidding to a halt, she tripped over her own feet and landed in a heap. Quickly rolling over onto her back, she scooted away from what had scared her so badly.

At first, she almost mistook the figure for a man. But the moment he tilted his head, she knew something was very, very wrong.

He was tall. Lean. His form was obscured beneath an

expensive, antique suit all in jet black. Shirt, coat, vest, tie, everything. His black hair made him a silhouette against the overly lit, florescent hallway. One of his arms was folded behind him.

But it wasn't his clothing or his hair that scared her.

It was the mask he wore.

Covering his entire face was a metal mask. Smooth, with only a single, circular hole over his right eye, with a straight line cutting down from the hole through the cheek and to the chin. It was black, like the rest of him. When he moved, the mask reflected a bit of the light.

He stared at her. Or at least, she assumed he did. She couldn't see anything beneath the hole in the mask except an inky nothingness.

The light overhead flickered.

And in the blink between the flashes... he was gone.

"What the... what the *fuck?*"

A strangled holler from back toward her office instantly told her that while the *second* monster had disappeared, the first one was still very, very much in the building. And still clearly very interested in killing her.

Lydia managed to get back up to her feet to start running again, just as the corpse was about to reach her. "Help!"

Footsteps were rounding the corner as other people in the building came to find the source of the screams. A mix of employees in lab coats and office garb gathered in the intersection of the hallway, eyes wide, as they had no idea what to expect, except fear. They were all coworkers she recognized but didn't know their names.

Lydia's running slammed her into one of them. The guy caught her and grasped her upper arms, keeping her from crashing them both into the wall.

She was shaking. She wanted to throw up. Wanted to cry. She turned down the hallway and saw the monster standing there in all his deathly glory. His white-and-blue translucent skin was blotchy under the overhead fluorescent lights. The creature seemed entirely indifferent to the dozens of circular wounds on his chest.

The impossible corpse stalked toward them down the hallway slowly. The cadaver had shut his mouth, hiding the too-long canines. He wasn't a shark going for the kill just yet; he was sizing up his prey. And they were prey. Lydia wanted to run, but somehow standing there with a small crowd felt safer. That, somehow, they would, by sheer numbers alone, be able to deal with the impossible monster coming down the hallway at them.

"What... the fuck... is that?" one of her building-mates exclaimed.

"Is this a prank?" another one asked.

"I wish," Lydia said quietly. She backed away from the monster. He had yet to take his eyes off her. All she wanted to do was hide behind the other people.

The monster rolled his shoulders, and someone in the small crowd groaned as there was an audible pop and a snap. And then... the walking cadaver laughed.

It was raspy, dry, and sounded like sandpaper rubbing on a brick. Gravelly and loose. Fear and dread welled in her as she retreated farther back away from the crowd. Adrenaline was screaming at her to run, and she wanted to listen.

"This is stupid," a woman in her forties said as she stepped forward. "All right, you've had your fun, you two." The woman walked halfway between the gathered crowd and the corpse and put her hands on her hips as if she were a schoolteacher scolding a pair of students on April Fools. "The makeup is very nicely done, but the lack of pants isn't terribly fair to the rest of us."

The woman turned to look back at Lydia with an accusatory glare, and Lydia was caught off guard once more as she realized the woman was blaming her as the other half of the prank. "N-no," Lydia stammered and shook her head. "This isn't—he isn't—"

"Then someone pulled off a great stunt on you," the woman said with a smile in her direction. "But the joke's over."

"It's not a—" Lydia tried to explain.

She never got the chance.

The monster was done listening. He ran down the remainder of the hallway and closed the distance between him and the older woman. The corpse slammed into her, grabbing her by the arms. In that instant, he opened his mouth, revealing the sharp and deadly canine teeth in his possession.

The crowd screamed and fell back against the wall as the monster's inertia was going to send him, and the older woman, crashing into the rest of them. They all recoiled and wound up as a tangled mess of people and limbs against the tile wall like a group throwing themselves clear of a car wreck.

But the impact never came.

The corpse was gone.

So was the woman.

The moment they had come close to the pack of people, the two of them merely... vanished. Gone.

"Jane?" a man asked. That must have been the older woman's name.

Nobody answered the call. They could see down the intersection of the hallways in all three directions. They had disappeared right before their eyes in a blink. No smoke, no mirrors, no moment of flickering lights. Just... gone.

"Jane!" the man shouted. No answer. The man turned to look at her, wide-eyed, as fear started to set in. "What's going on?" he demanded.

"I don't know," Lydia said breathlessly, her heart pounding in her ears. She didn't know what a panic attack felt like, but she was wondering if she was getting close to one. "I just—he was in a bag, I unzipped him, and..." She trailed off, unable to finish. *I was doing an autopsy, and like everyone's worst nightmare, he got up and tried to kill me.*

That was what she wanted to say. But somehow, self-preservation kicked in. If she said that, they'd label her an accomplice because the other option—that it was true—wasn't possible.

Never mind the fact they had just seen a naked dead man and a woman disappear right in front of their eyes. If she added to that ridiculousness by saying the man was not wearing makeup and that he was actually a monster, it'd all be pinned on her.

Not to mention that the dead man had a mark on his face bearing a substantial similarity to the one she mysteriously woke up with this morning.

She just shook her head uselessly and hoped the man would pin her silence on her panic. It wasn't too far from the truth.

The man seemed to buy it, at least. "Jane!" he shouted again and put both of his hands through his hair. "Oh God. We have to call the cops."

The cops just made things worse.

Not because the cops weren't trying to help, mind you. They were. But even they didn't know what to do.

Once the security footage was fetched and played back on the monitor, the cops instantly brought all the witnesses and sat them down in a room. Which didn't feel like normal protocol, and she couldn't help but wonder why.

It wasn't long before she got her answer.

A naked dead man grabbing a woman and disappearing in a single frame of a film would have been one thing. That would have been hard enough for them to explain.

But it was far, far worse than that.

There was no monster corpse on the film.

The rest of the events played out exactly as they should have. They all went through the motions like the terrible CGI monster hadn't been added into the frame yet. Maybe the cops would have written it off as Lydia being on drugs except for one thing—Jane.

It was the moment when Jane was yanked off her feet and carried by some invisible force, crashing into the rest of the group, that left everyone staring at the film wide-eyed. That was when the real questioning began.

They split them all off into separate rooms. Each of them was grilled by a cop, asking for a description of precisely what had happened. Lydia knew she was in for the worst of it, as she had been the lucky winner and had been the monster's first target.

"So," the cop started and sat down in a chair across from her in an office they had borrowed. They were questioning them all here and not back at the precinct, in the hopes that they'd be done with this before the end of the day, and Lydia and the others could all go home. "Run through it again with me."

Lydia had told them exactly what happened twice already. But, she dutifully went through the boring parts of her day— *minus* the tattoo that honestly she'd half forgotten about by now and the creepy guy in all black that was probably a hallucination.

The cop nodded at all the mundane bits. "Then what happened?"

"I was pulling out all the buckshot when he, uh…" Lydia paused and looked down in her coffee, feeling the tightness in her throat start up again. Just the memory of that man sitting up on the table made her mouth go dry and her hands start shaking. "I swear—I swear I didn't have anything to do with this."

"Hey, hey…" The cop—Officer Malley was his name—was doing his best to calm her down. "We aren't saying you did. You aren't a suspect. We just don't have any answers, and we're trying to figure this out and find your coworker."

"The corpse just... got up. I screamed, I fell over... I grabbed my phone and ran the hell out of there as fast as I could. He kept screaming at me."

"So, from the tapes, you're just standing there, working on... nothing at all," Malley said with a sigh. "But what's weird is we can hear him. We have his voice on the tape. We can see things fall over on their own."

"*That's* what's weird about all this?" Lydia couldn't hide her sarcasm. She was exhausted.

"Well, hey, I mean," the cop stammered, then shrugged, "it's all weird."

The door to the room swung open, and an older cop walked in. This one wasn't in full street garb. Probably a detective. "Everyone's stories all match up. We've swept the building, no sign of Mrs. Tiel." Jane's last name, Lydia figured. "We can't hold anyone without a warrant, and I need to wait for digital forensics to answer their damn messages." He grumbled down at his own cell phone. "Look, I know tomorrow's a holiday," the detective said, tiredly looking up from the screen to Lydia, "but I really need you to stay in town."

"No problem. I'll be here." It wasn't like she ever went anywhere for Thanksgiving, anyway. Her family all lived in Seattle, so traditionally she just took an extended Christmas break to go hang out with them. Nick and Lydia were going to have a "Friendsgiving" or whatever people called it. It was their own personal tradition for the past few years.

"Good. Thank you. You're free to go." The detective was clearly asking her to leave the room so he could talk to Officer Malley. Fine by her. Picking up her stuff, she headed out.

Free to go.

Why did that feel like a lie?

* * *

When Lydia found Nick on the sidewalk outside the building, she didn't say anything. If she opened her mouth, she'd lose her tenuous grasp on the tears she'd been fighting all afternoon. So instead, she just hugged him. God damn it, she needed a hug right now. He clutched her tightly as she rested her head on his shoulder.

They stood like that for a while, before she finally pushed away and nodded weakly in thanks. She really did seriously need that after the corpse, after the cops, after everything. Nick hadn't been questioned, but he worked in security. He knew all about what had happened.

As she pulled away, she felt something on his side under the zip-up hoodie he was wearing. Something hard was strapped to his side. "Nick? Are you wearing a gun?" she asked warily, shooting him an incredulous glance.

Nick had a license to carry a concealed weapon. He was a security guard in a dangerous area of town. There were handguns for the security guards in the office that they signed for when they clocked in and out of work. None went off the property. Ever. And yet, here one was.

"No one'll notice until Monday. It's a holiday, and in all the fuss, I can say I forgot it because of what happened." Nick shrugged. "Walter'll write me up and forget anything happened." Walter, Nick's boss, was notoriously lax.

"You stole it."

"I'm *borrowing* it. You got attacked, Lyd!" he insisted. "And I'm trained. I know what I'm doing."

"Great. Just don't shoot me." Lydia pinched the bridge of her nose and tried to fight off a headache she felt edging in at the back of her skull.

"You all right?" he asked, probably knowing it was a stupid question, but having to ask it anyway.

"No. I need a cocktail. Beer isn't going to do it this time," she muttered as they began to walk down the street. The fact that they needed to gather up after everything was over and talk it through was just understood between them. Besides, she was starving. Her hands were shaking. Partially from the day's events, but also because she hadn't had anything to eat except a package of crackers the police had provided to her a few hours ago, and it was now well past eight in the evening.

"I saw the tapes," Nick said quietly. "They said a corpse attacked you...?"

"Yeah." Lydia shoved her hands into her coat pockets. She wanted to hide the rest of her in there if only she could. "It got up. Chased me. Grabbed that woman and just... poof."

"You sure he was dead?" When she glared at him hard enough to put a hole in his head, he raised his hands defensively. "Hey. Hey. I had to ask."

Lydia rubbed her hand across her face. "The cops asked the same thing. Three times. I'm not the best at my job, but I know when somebody's dead."

"I know, I know." Nick bumped his elbow into her arm. It was his way of apologizing, in his I-don't-ever-actually-say-sorry kind of way. Lydia had grown up with one vaguely douchebag-y older brother, and now she joked that she had wound up with the second one in Nick.

All her other friends wondered why she and Nick weren't a thing. By his own words, he wasn't interested, and neither was she. They were family to each other, close friends and nothing more. They understood each other and their weird quirks.

The two of them made it to their favorite spot to drink and sat in the restaurant section. Usually, they just hunkered down at a corner of the bar. But this time, they ordered some food along with drinks. Lydia got her favorite, an old fashioned, deciding she needed a treat since she had been chased by a homicidal monster that day and all. God, it sounded stupid even saying it to herself in her head.

It made the tattoo on her arm seem a lot less weird by comparison. It was incredible how context was king.

"Are you okay?" Nick scratched at his collarbone idly.

"I don't know." She ran her hand through her hair and let out a small breath she hadn't realized she'd been holding. It felt like every little sound, every tiny plink of glassware or silverware, was going to send her jumping out of the window in a panic. She didn't think of herself as a jumpy person, but here she was, proving that theory false.

They were both quiet, and she picked at the part of her sleeve over the tattoo, unable to help but dwell on it. Lydia didn't even notice that Nick was shifting uncomfortably in his seat. It wasn't until he cleared his throat that she realized he'd been trying, nervously, to get her attention.

"What's up?" She raised an eyebrow.

"Look, I didn't want to bring this up earlier. You've had some weird shit happen to you today, and you don't need to deal with my weird shit," Nick rambled.

"It's fine. I don't think my day could get any worse. Go for it."

Nick began to unzip his hoodie and pull it away from his neck. "I just... I gotta tell somebody. I've been scouring the internet about it all day."

"Look, your rash is between you and your doctor." She smirked.

"Yeah, yeah." He dismissed her joke with a snicker, enjoying her crude humor. "But what in the actual fuck is *this,* though?" He pulled the edge of his T-shirt away from his neck.

There, just below the collarbone on one side, was a mark. About the size of a quarter. It looked like some messed-up alchemical symbol. A four with two dash lines through it. Black ink. Like a perfect, single-line tattoo. It would take an artist maybe five minutes to etch it onto his skin. But impossible for someone to get magically without them realizing or remembering it.

Lydia felt her face go pale. Felt all the color drain out of her face like someone had pulled the tap for the second time that day.

"I know you think I'm nuts." Nick shook his head. "I know you're going to say I just got trashed and don't remember getting it. But I-I—" He paused to swallow the lump in his throat. "I swear I didn't get a tattoo, and not last night. Last night I just smoked a joint and went to bed and I didn't—I don't know what the *fuck* is going on, Lyd!" Nick's voice turned higher and strained as his eyes went wide.

Silently, as actions spoke louder than the words she didn't know how to form, Lydia rolled up her sleeve to her elbow and put her arm down on the table, palm up. Showing him that she, too, had a mark. When he saw it, he grabbed her arm and ran his thumb over her tattoo as if he was trying to wipe it off. As if confirming it matched his. Maybe not in shape, but certainly in style.

She didn't know what to say, except, "I believe you."

* * *

Edu gripped the hilt of his sword as he looked down over this human city. It had been several years since the last Ceremony of the Fall, and over a hundred years since he had returned to this plane.

It had always been his opinion that human society grew too slowly. Although now, perhaps he would have to amend his previous beliefs.

The human world had changed so dramatically in such a seemingly short period of time. Buildings were taller, made of glass and steel and not mounds of brick and mortar. Such construction still remained, lingering in the architecture of a previous time, mixing with the buildings of all the generations that stretched back into its lineage.

This was a young city, as this world went, merely a few hundred years old. It had not yet resorted so fully to ransacking its own footprint to rebuild as many others had turned to in their time. In his home, they could build on and on, spread outward into the void, and expand to their heart's content.

Rather, that was how their world was *meant* to work.

Those days were dead and gone. Lying in the lake with all the rest.

But Edu had not come to this fledgling city to reminisce and philosophize upon human nature and his own shrinking world. He had come, for it was time for the Fall, and he would not miss it for all the glory of Under. There were few things he relished so keenly as the hunt.

For when the Ceremony of the Fall began... there was prey to be gathered.

THREE

Even if it made her feel vaguely like she was going to throw up, Lydia was happy for the food in her stomach. And the alcohol. Mostly, it was probably the alcohol that was making her a little queasy. But hell if it wasn't worth it. The slight hum she got from the booze made the whole day so much more tolerable.

Lydia had told Nick about the marks on the corpse's face, the walking cadaver with the sharp, far-too-long canines. Nick had, of course, said the thing that she was refusing to even speak silently in her mind.

"Wait. The guy was a vampire?"

"No. No, that shit isn't real." She put her head in her hands. "Vampires aren't real."

"But he was a corpse. He was dead. And then he wasn't. And he had fangs. We both have tattoos we don't remember getting. Ones that matched the ones you say this guy had on his face. I'm willing to go on a little suspension of disbelief here." He tapped his finger on the table as if that'd help prove his point.

"Say you're right. Say he was a vampire." Fuck, she couldn't believe she was actually entertaining the notion. "If he did have the same style marks on his face, what the hell does that mean? What're we now, under attack by some weird supernatural cult?"

"I don't know." Nick sighed. "But it's gotta be connected. It's gotta be. It's too impossible for it to be a coincidence."

Nick was right. The idea that somehow the two events weren't connected was even dumber. Somehow the mark on her arm and the one on Nick's collarbone were related to the it-was-totally-a-vampire *monster* she wound up with on her slab.

After dinner and drinks, and not wanting to pay for a cab back after the last T stopped running, they paid up and started the walk home. Nick, even if he didn't admit it, was starting to look more and more worried as the night went on. He had asked to crash on her sofa, and she was more than happy to say yes. It was that or sleep with the lights on. Hell, she might sleep with the lights on anyway.

It was about halfway home that they both abruptly stopped walking.

A man was standing in the middle of the road.

Well, she assumed it was a man.

It also might have been a bus, if his size was any indication.

Whoever it was, he was in full armor. Full, honest-to-God plate armor. Like something out of a movie, it covered every inch of his body from head to toe. Unlike museum pieces, the sections and plates looked like they had been made of hunks of weird stone or maybe black lava rock, not steel or metal. The plates connected in a nonsensical way that mimicked how plates on an insect's exoskeleton might join together.

The armor was pointed, vicious, and was clearly designed to intimidate, not just to protect whoever wore it. And it looked incredibly successful on both counts.

The man was huge. He wore a full helmet that obscured his features entirely. It stretched up over his head and tapered off into two great horns that looked like they belonged to a dragon, twisted and cruel. The horns and the thickness of his armor obscured his actual height, but from the pavement to the top, he might have been eight feet total.

Even without the armor, he was broad and had to be incredibly muscular with how much that armor must weigh. The man was carrying a sword that looked like it might be four feet in length with one hand. The gauntlet that grasped it was clawed and pointed like everything else about him.

Etched into every surface of his armor seemed to be writing. It was identical to the kind they had on them now as tattoos.

"Master Edu bids you good evening. He wishes you well. We mean you no harm, and we ask you to come with us."

He wasn't alone.

Standing behind him and to the side was a woman. Lydia hadn't noticed her at first, as she was too busy gaping at the giant man in the plate armor. The woman who had spoken had long, black hair that reached to her waist. She wore a crimson dress that draped around her like layers of silk. It was split down the front to her navel and wouldn't have been accepted anywhere as real clothing. But it didn't seem to bother her at all.

And the dress wasn't the weirdest thing about her.

Over the top half of her face was a solid crimson mask. There were no holes for the eyes, and it obscured everything from her nose up. Across one section of it was a jagged-edged spiral, etched into the surface and inked gold that glinted in the streetlights.

She was the one who had spoken, and her full red lips were curved in a gentle smile as she stood there, hands folded peacefully in front of her. She was a stark contrast to the armored monolith she was standing next to. Her expression—what Lydia could see of it anyway—wasn't mean. Just passive and almost... like she pitied Lydia and Nick.

The few people who had been on the street were quick to

turn around and go the other way. The two bizarre figures seemed not to care about anybody else.

"Nick..." Lydia took a step back, accidentally bumping into him. The impact seemed to shake him out of it, and he grabbed her hand. "We need to go," she muttered.

"Master Edu insists that running is not advisable." The woman's red lips twisted up in a slightly broader smile. "Although it is enjoyable."

That was the last straw.

Nick and Lydia turned, and for the second time in one day, Lydia ran for her life. Nick had to let go of her so they didn't drag each other down over themselves. They tore down the street as fast as they could. Lydia wasn't a trained runner. She went to the gym twice a week to not be a lump, sure, but she mostly did weight machines. Lydia hated running. Now, she scolded herself for not having stuck to cardio. It certainly would've come in handy right now.

How far they went, she couldn't say, before Nick took a sharp right down an alley. Lydia missed the turn and skidded to a halt. She quickly turned back up the way they had come to catch up with her friend.

No. Not possible.

How could something that big move that fast?

There he was—the man in the armor—barely twenty feet away. He was standing stock still, watching her with his head tilted slightly to the side as if curious about them. But he looked like he hadn't moved at all to get there. Meanwhile, she was a sweaty, out-of-breath mess.

The man in the armor was looking at her with the empty, black, and jagged eye sockets of its helm fixed straight on her. Its mask was sculpted to look like a dragon—or a skull. Or both, maybe. Nothing was visible underneath, like there might not be anyone inside.

Like the freak in all black that I saw. Maybe she hadn't hallucinated him, after all.

If the man's mask was supposed to be terrifying, it worked. Lydia screamed and turned to run again. She made it about three steps before something massive snatched her arm. The sudden stopping of her momentum would have knocked her to the ground if whatever grabbed her hadn't picked her up off her feet and set her back down like she was a child's toy.

It was like being stuck in a vise, but she thrashed and struggled anyway. The armored man had crossed twenty feet of distance inhumanly fast. Worse, it moved almost silently for something wearing what amounted to a tank. A heavy gauntlet had wrapped around her upper arm and was keeping her from escaping.

"Let me go!" Lydia screamed.

The man just looked down at Lydia, silent and foreboding. It tilted its head the other direction, like a German shepherd, trying to figure her out. No amount of thrashing on her part was even budging the man. She kicked at his leg with her boot, but she felt like she was kicking a rock. He didn't move. All she got in response was a stab of pain that shot up her leg.

The creature lifted its other hand, to do what, she didn't know, but stopped as someone shouted from behind him.

"Hey, asshole!"

The monolithic creature turned its head back up the street. There stood Nick, the source of the interruption. He had his gun raised. "Let her go."

The creature didn't. In fact, the man didn't move. Just looked at Nick, still as a statue.

"Second chance," Nick warned.

The creature turned toward Nick, dragging Lydia with him. It reached its free hand out in front of him and down, palm tilted forward, as if to grasp something. A strange red light crackled between the fingers of his gauntleted hand. It almost looked like electricity, arcing between the creature's claws. Lydia couldn't help but whimper in fear as the power grew, and the sword she had seen him carrying earlier appeared in the monster's hand. One second, his hand was empty, and the next, the wicked and vicious blade was in his grasp.

To anyone else, it would have been a two-handed weapon. For this guy, he held it with one like it was nothing. And he had summoned it from thin air. The monster tightened its grasp around the hilt of the sword and held it pointed toward Nick. The answer to his challenge.

If Nick wanted to fight, this guy was game.

"Oh, fuck—" Nick took aim. Lydia would have been afraid Nick might hit her except for the fact that he really was an excellent shot. The monster in armor was also the size of a small truck, so would be hard to miss.

Nick fired off several shots, the sound echoing off the buildings in the alley.

The monster stood there unflinching as each one seemed to bounce off harmlessly. As if nothing had happened.

Lydia ducked reflexively as she heard the bullets ricochet off the armor and bounce into nearby objects. The window of a nearby parked car shattered. Nick hadn't missed. The fucker was literally *bulletproof.*

"Run, Nick! Just go!" Maybe he had time to escape. Maybe he could save himself.

The armored monster let out a low growl, the first sound she had heard from him. It hadn't been keen on Nick opening fire, apparently. Suddenly, she was on the ground. It had tossed her to the floor like a discarded toy. She let out an *umph* as she impacted the pavement.

The armored man was now walking toward Nick. If her friend hadn't managed to hurt the man, at least he managed to annoy it. Nick quickly realized the predicament he was now in, and he took a step back. "Uh, hey, let's talk this through, okay? Who are you? What do you want?"

The creature didn't answer. Instead, he just kept slowly walking toward Nick. The armored man was in no hurry as if the monolith was so sure of his success. And so far, Nick and Lydia posed him no threat. Not even a gun did any damage or even seemed to slow him down.

In a sudden blur of motion, the creature dashed forward faster than should have been possible. Faster than Lydia could track. He swiped a claw at Nick and slapped the gun out of his hand, sending it skittering down the sidewalk.

Nick screamed and staggered backward. "Run, Lyd!" He took off down the alleyway he had disappeared down the first time.

It was run—or give up. There weren't any other options. Lydia scrambled to her feet and grabbed the gun. Maybe if they split up, they could confuse it and get away. At least one of them would escape, right? Lydia took off in the other direction.

She made it about two blocks before she had to stop and catch her breath. Lydia leaned against the wall of the alleyway she had ducked down and bent over to rest her arms on her knees. She tried to keep her dinner down and take air in. Shit, Lydia needed air. Holy hell... what should she do? Call the cops? Even if they didn't believe her, it couldn't hurt. Either the monster would vanish, and she'd be safe—or they'd take one look at it and call the SWAT team. Or the fucking National Guard.

A shadow fell over Lydia. Something tall enough to blot out the streetlamp about thirty feet away. Lydia knew it wasn't going to be Nick. Looking up, her sense of dread was confirmed. Now she knew which one of them the man in armor had chased.

Her.

He walked up to her, still taking his time. When she turned

to run, he was suddenly standing right in front of her. She added that to the list of crazy impossible shit she'd seen today. One massive gauntlet closed around her arm again and squeezed, just hard enough to hurt a little.

It was a warning, clear as day. He could break her arm in two if he clenched down. He wouldn't even need to try to snap her like a twig. If she ran again, he would make her regret it.

He pulled her away from the wall. For a beat, she stared at him, getting her first up-close view of the monster. The man underneath was easily seven feet tall, judging by where his shoulders were. Where the mask had a gap in it, she could see his neck, clothed in black.

So, there *was* somebody in there. At least it wasn't empty armor running around trying to kill her. That was a plus. Somehow that made it less spooky, that he wasn't just some empty piece of furniture stomping around. If he had a neck with black clothing, there was somebody inside.

His neck.

Somewhere, all those years watching horror movies finally served a purpose. Somewhere, deep down, pulling from her fear, or adrenaline—or simply the raw need to survive—the strength to do something smart for once.

Lifting Nick's gun, she put the end of it point-blank against the gap in the man's armor where his mask ended and his shoulder armor began. She angled it up under his chin, which was easy to do since she was so much shorter than he was. Before the man could react, she pulled the trigger.

Lydia had seen a lot of gore in her days.

Really, there was a lot of gore in her life.

From the horror movies she watched willingly, or the dead bodies that wound up on her slab, or her years as an EMT and her continued service as a first responder.

She'd seen a lot of gross, torn up people, including that guy who had disrespected an industrial lathe when she had been an EMT.

But the spray of blood that hit her was enough to send her dinner right back up to her throat. This was different. This was fresh. This was real.

And this was her fault.

Lydia stood stock still, unsure of what to do or even to think, as she felt the warmth of the blood against the skin of her hand and face.

After what seemed like an eternity, the man collapsed to his knees, his grip on her arm slackening as he fell. He lingered there for a moment before falling to his side with a thud and the rattle of armor.

Lydia backed up slowly against the wall and swallowed hard, trying to keep herself from losing her dinner all over the ground as she felt the warm liquid on her start to ooze. She wiped away at it frantically and realized her hands were shaking violently.

I just shot a man. I just shot a man. I just shot a man.

All Lydia wanted in the world was to be away from here. To be home and in bed. To let this all be fake, a fever dream. Maybe she was in a coma, and this was summoned forth out of her cancer-ridden brain.

Lydia punched herself in the thigh, trying to wake herself up. Nope. That had just hurt, and she was still here. *I just shot a man.* The thought kept going in her head, threatening to drive everything else away and push her into a straight-up, all-out breakdown.

No, idiot! No! Panic later. Solve the problem first. Panic later. Some part of her EMT training was kicking in. Panic later. She could panic later.

Lydia flipped the safety on the gun and tucked it into her bag. She rummaged around and found a napkin from her breakfast coffee that she had shoved in there. Desperately, she tried to wipe away the splatter that must still be on her face and her arms. She had to get home. She couldn't take the T like this, couldn't call a cab.

Walking home, it was. At least it was late and dark. Maybe she could go unseen. Lydia walked hurriedly out of the alley and toward home. It'd take her an hour or two to make the long trek, but it wasn't like she had a choice.

Yanking her phone out of her pocket, she called Nick. It rang a few times, then went to voice mail. She didn't bother leaving him one. Instead, she hung up and dialed again.

I just shot a man. A man in full plate armor, who was trying to do... who knew what. Lydia tried to trace through what had happened, working backward. The woman in the red dress and the strange crimson mask. She had said that "Master Edu"—the man in the armor—had asked them to come with him.

Was he trying to abduct them? Why? To where? Who was he? What did this have to do with the mark on her arm or the corpse who had attacked her? Edu was dead now. She had shot him point blank and up into his skull, after all, so at least he wouldn't be a problem anymore. What about the woman in the red dress, with the freaky mask?

Eight phone calls to Nick and no answer, so she finally gave up. She'd try again in an hour or two. Something about the drudge of walking and the time alone made it sink in. All of it, all at once, settled on her like the impact of a brick. Without Nick there to help carry the weight, she felt the tears she had been holding back all day finally win out and run down her face.

I just shot a man.

At least nobody was around who might see her, bloody and crying, walking through the streets at night by herself. Lydia wiped at the tears with the napkin and let them run their course.

Now, the task was to accept everything as fact.

Lydia had a tattoo that was impossible—fine, but it was still there. Fact.

She had been attacked by a corpse of a man who had risen from the dead. Unlikely, but fact.

Lydia and Nick had been pursued by a monster in a full suit of armor who could move faster than she could see. Absurd, but fact.

And she'd shot him. Fact.

All she could hope was that Nick was okay—that he'd just dropped his phone. That whatever was hunting them hadn't sent more people after the two of them.

A sudden realization came to her that sparked both fear and dread in the same moment.

Was it these marks that they were hunting?

She rolled up her coat and looked down at the little tattoo on her arm and let out a wavering breath. These marks were the only things connecting it all. The only thing linking her to the corpse and the monstrous man in the armor. If they were hunting the marks, then... there was one thing she could try.

There was one way she knew that would get rid of it for sure.

Lydia let out an audible groan.

Oh, this was going to hurt.

FOUR

Breathe in, breathe out.

It wouldn't be so awful. Right?

There wasn't another option. It was this, or do nothing, and nothing was worse. Nothing was admitting she was helpless —and she hated feeling helpless, more than anything else.

Lydia sat at her kitchen counter and looked down at the mark on her left forearm. It had been surreal but harmless until two different monsters with matching symbols had chased her. Lydia was resting her arm on one of the junky bath towels she kept shoved on a shelf.

They always came in handy. You never knew when you needed a bath towel that you didn't care if you had to throw out when you were done with it. Spills, leaks, messy projects...

Home surgery.

Y'know.

Normal shit.

All her first aid equipment was scattered around her on the counter. She had a sizable collection from her EMT days. It was hard to throw that kind of thing out.

Lydia sighed heavily and reached for the metal handle

sticking out of the cup of rubbing alcohol on the counter. Pulling her little hobby knife out of the glass, she looked at it and let out a groan of dismay. No chickening out. This had to be done.

If she cut this thing off her, there was a small chance she'd be safe. In theory. It was the only theory she had, so she was going to have to go with it.

Lydia had already swabbed her arm and tied a tourniquet around her upper forearm above the tattoo, just in case. It wasn't near any major arteries, and she only had to go down the tiniest amount, but she might slip. Lydia even had a cookie tray all set and sterilized for her used equipment—and bits of flesh. That reminder of what she was going to do made her stomach flip, and she wished she had drunk more at the bar earlier. Finally, she put the edge of the blade to her skin.

"*Fuck*—" Lydia made it about a quarter of the way around the symbol before she had to stop, her eyes were watering so badly. She slammed the knife down onto the cookie sheet and punched herself in the thigh a few times, gagging in pain.

Lydia picked up a washcloth and rubbed at her face, then decided to stick it into her mouth to bite down on and muffle her hollering from the neighbors if she had to resort to that. Picking up the knife, resumed the cut where she left off.

It got less painful as she went because the nerves in her arms couldn't scream much louder. At least she knew what she was doing. At least she did this kind of shit for a living. Oh man, at least the dead people didn't feel it, though.

This... oh God, she was going to be sick.

Too bad she had to do this with her off hand.

Standing from the counter, she tore the washcloth from her mouth and doubled over the sink. Retching into it, she ran the cold water and the garbage disposal before retching again. Cold shivers ran up her spine as the adrenaline—whatever was left of it in her system—rampaged through her. She cupped the cold water and rinsed out her mouth, then ran more cold water over her face, trying to cool herself down.

Okay. Okay. Not much more to go. She could do this. Lydia put the bloody and sliced up part of her forearm under the cold water and let out a breath of relief as it poured across her agonized skin. She had finished cutting around the tattoo, and now all that was left was to... rip it off.

No big deal.

Perfectly normal.

Skin peeled. It was a thing. Lydia had done it to hundreds of corpses before. She'd just never done it to a living person before. It was the same thing, right? Totally. Totally! It'd be fine. Just fine.

Don't chicken out now. You're so close.

Sitting back down on the stool, she reached into the cup of rubbing alcohol and picked up the small pair of forceps that had been soaking in it.

Like a Band-Aid, right?

Just like a Band-Aid.

Lydia wormed the edge of one half of the forceps' teeth into her skin.

One.

Two.

* * *

Aon had not expected haunting a young mortal woman to be nearly as entertaining as it turned out to be. He had been missing out on centuries of enjoyment, it seemed. And this young woman—Lydia, it seemed was her name—was quite the source of amusement.

More than once, he had found himself laughing in joy, wishing she could have heard his appreciation for her antics.

First, he had watched her utterly debase one of the House

of Blood's minions who had been foolishly caught in the blast of a mortal's gun. It seemed her career involved the study of corpses. Watching her idly fish each small metal bullet from the man whose body was recovering from the injury had been delicious—for he knew what was surely to follow. Each moment a step closer to the inevitable.

Her fear had been delectable. A true masterpiece of terror. He could not resist a front row seat. And when she had glimpsed his voyeurism, even for just a second of peering through the veil that separated them, his desire had roared to life in a sudden bonfire.

Aon had thought for a moment that his entertainment would cease there. But it seemed Lydia was *full* of surprises. The whole night had been wonderful! He even, strangely, enjoyed eavesdropping upon her conversation with the little pedant boy she must call a friend. If only because their false sense of security made what followed all the more wonderful.

How he had howled in laughter when she had shot Edu! The bastard King of Flames deserved nothing more than to be brought low—*and defeated*—by a little human woman an eighth his size! He had applauded her efforts, though she had not heard his call for an encore performance.

Now, he found himself here, in her piteous abode, gazing down at her unconscious body on the floor. Blood slowly seeping from the hole in her arm that she had carved herself. He crouched down beside her, studying her.

He had watched her recent effort to escape with abject fascination. What a *treat* for him to behold.

Not many he knew would have the wherewithal to do such a task—and his kind healed from even the most grievous of wounds. To be mortal, and to suffer such harm willingly, spoke to both her resolve and her desperation in equal measure. He had shattered many an immortal with far less than what she inflicted upon herself.

She was not one who would fall victim to the world if she could help it. What a goddess she would become in Under before long. *I can only pray to the Ancients you fall into the House of Shadows. It is clear you are meant for me.*

"You and I... we will have so much fun together." Reaching down, he gave in to his temptation and let his flesh-and-blood hand trail through her soft hair. He would take this unbreakable thing and show her the face of true suffering.

But, like fine wine, all things were to be enjoyed in their time. Her little device that she used to communicate with people made a racket from the countertop. Lydia stirred, coughing and moaning in pain. Aon took the cue and retreated into the shadows of the room, content to watch.

For now.

* * *

Lydia woke up with a groan as her phone buzzed, the ring tone waking her up out of the darkness. The last thing she remembered, she had been—

Fuck.

Right.

That.

Lifting her arm, she saw a bloody circle there, oozing up onto her elbow and the floor. A crimson ring, the size of a nickel—and no tattoo.

She must have ripped it off and, well, passed out like a champ.

All right, fine, she'd accept that without any injury to her pride. Most people didn't do at-home tattoo removal. Pushing up to her feet, she gripped the edge of the kitchen sink counter hard with her other hand to steady herself.

Her phone had stopped ringing. It was probably Nick. She'd deal with him in a moment, when she wasn't bleeding everywhere. Step one—rinse off her arm and make sure the damn black ink mark wasn't still there under the blood. This time, as the cold water touched her skin, she screwed her eyes shut and swore loudly, pounding her other fist into the counter repeatedly to try to distract herself from the stinging pain.

Finally, when she felt like she could see straight, she looked down at her arm. She could see the red patch underneath, and thankfully, there was no black ink in the skin there.

Success!

The bandage she wrapped around it instantly soaked through red. The wound would ooze for a while. Lydia would have to treat it like a nasty burn. Maybe she'd scar, not that she really honestly cared. She'd shot a man in a full suit of armor and been chased by a dead man today.

A scar was not really on her radar of things to care about.

Okay. The deed was done. The thing was gone. She found the section of skin on the floor where she had passed out, and she stuck it down the garbage disposal and ran it.

Take that, evil, weird tattoo thing!

Was now the time for another drink? It was three in the morning. And she had just done home surgery. Wandering to her fridge, she opened it, and then she saw something on her right forearm.

There was only one word that came to mind for what she saw. One four-letter word that she screamed loud enough to wake the neighbors. She didn't care.

On her right forearm—not the left one, with the bleeding hole in it—was a small, nickel-sized mark. A backward N with a spiral cutting it in half.

It was the same symbol.

Identical.

Just on the other arm now.

Lydia felt herself crying again, this time not out of pain, but out of frustration. That was supposed to work. The stupid thing wasn't just supposed to reappear! That wasn't possible. None of this was. It might be time to chuck what she considered possible out the window.

When her phone buzzed violently on the counter, she jolted in surprise. Looking at her phone, she saw it was now half past four. She'd been unconscious for a little over an hour.

Answering the phone, she put it on speaker. "Hey. You okay?"

"Yeah, I am. I'm okay. I got away. I dropped my phone, and it took me this long to trace back and find it. Are you okay?" he asked, equally as excitable. "How'd you get away?"

"I shot the guy." She ran a hand through her hair, combing it back. "I got it in under his armor and put a bullet in his head."

"You *what?*" he said through a laugh. "No way. Holy fuck, good job, Lyd! Where are you now?"

"Home. I tried to cut the symbol off my arm, to see if that would work. To see if that's how they're finding us. Sorry I missed your first call, I was... uh... dealing with the mess." She looked down at the spot on her arm, still soaking through the bandage.

"You... you what? Jesus Christ, you're kidding me. Are you okay?"

"I'm okay, it just—shit, that sucked. And it didn't work." Lydia winced as she poked the bandage from her arm. Good God, it stung.

"What do you mean, it didn't work?"

"I mean the symbol just appeared on my *other* fucking arm as soon as I was done." Saying it made it real, and she let out a wavering sigh. She went to the freezer for an ice pack. Maybe that'd help the stinging.

Nick was silent on the other side, no doubt trying to reconcile her news with the reality they both believed they had been living in until this point. "Hey. We should circle up. Let's meet halfway over by Rogers Street and wait for the Starbucks to open."

Rogers Street Park, with its two baseball diamonds, sat about halfway between Nick's apartment and hers. They'd met there a few times before walking for coffee. It was still early, and Starbucks wouldn't open for another hour. But circling up sounded good, and God knew she wanted to talk to someone about the fact that she straight up had to shoot a man.

"Sure," Lydia said. Starbucks was calling her name. It was even pumpkin spice latte season. "Twenty minutes?" She'd need to change and wanted to take a shower.

"Twenty minutes, Lyd. Be safe, please."

* * *

The streets were just as silent as they were when she walked home when she found Nick sitting on a bench by one of the baseball diamonds. Nick raised his head. He looked exhausted, and she was sure she didn't look much better. He stood to greet her and reached out to hug her. Lydia hugged him tightly and let out a wavering breath. They had been chased by a monster who had nearly done God knew what to them.

"Hey, you should take this back." Lydia pushed away from him gently and reached into her bag. She handed him the gun, making sure for the twentieth time that the safety was still clicked on.

Nick laughed and shot her a lopsided grin. "You sure? You did better with it than I did. Did you seriously kill him? How?" He didn't seem like he believed her. Honestly, she didn't blame him.

"There was a guy under all that armor. I saw his neck, and... I went for it." She shrugged. It didn't feel impressive. It had felt horrifying and disgusting, even if the guy had it coming. Even if the monster of a man had probably not really been human.

"Shit, Lyd."

"I don't want to do that again." Lydia felt the bile rise in her throat. Nick pulled her into another tight hug, and she let her head rest on his shoulder once more.

"It's going to be fine."

"It's really probably not."

"No, but that's what you say to people."

Lydia shoved Nick and laughed. "You suck at this."

He only offered his stupid grin again and shrugged. "I—"

Someone cut him off.

"I deeply commend you both on your efforts thus far."

Lydia nearly jumped out of her skin. Whirling, she saw a man standing there, about ten feet away. He had appeared from nowhere; neither of them had seen or heard the man approach.

It wasn't the giant monster of a man in armor, and it wasn't the woman in red. This man was tall and thin. He wore all white. His clothing was dated and looked almost... Victorian. He even had a pocket watch tucked into a double-breasted vest. It seemed painfully familiar in style to the corpse that had chased her.

His hair was nearly white, as was his skin. Standing with his hands clasped behind his back, the man had the appearance of a marble statue or a ghost. He was beautiful like a statue of a saint or an angel in a church—cold and inhuman. His eyes were a pale ice blue that almost completed the illusion of him being made of stone.

He bowed, folding an arm in front of him as he did. "I fear your attempts at escape will be fruitless from here forward."

"Who the *fuck* are you?" Nick drew the gun back out of the holster where it had been for about sixty seconds. He clicked the safety off. "You aren't wearing armor. I'm betting you bleed, just like the other guy."

"I do." The man seemed entirely unalarmed at the loaded pistol pointed at his face. "You will find that your bullets will have trouble landing all the same. Please, lower your weapon and come with me." The man reached out a hand. As if they were going to walk up to him and blindly agree.

Maybe he was hoping they would. There was a forlorn look to his features, Lydia realized, a strange kind of sadness. It was so etched into him, it was hard to see at first.

Nick answered the strange man's threat with "challenge accepted" and fired off two rounds from the gun. But as the strange man predicted, neither bullet found its target.

He'd vanished into thin air.

The mystery of where he went didn't last long, barely a fraction of a second. Nick squawked in surprise as the man reappeared beside them. Before Nick could react, the man grasped the gun around the barrel and pointed it upward.

The man's smile was faint. "You will wake the neighborhood."

Nick let go of the gun and staggered back, knocking Lydia to the ground as he did. Nick managed to stay on his feet but wound up almost sitting on the bench in a tangled mass of terrified limbs.

The man merely held the gun in his hand, palm up, and extended it out in front of him. The gun in his hand... *melted.* Heated up to red and dripped from his fingers in molten drabs of steel that hit the ground with a hiss.

"Oh God!" Nick staggered back farther away from the molten blob on the ground as it oozed out from where it had hit the dirt and began to sear and singe the grass.

Lydia had managed to make it back to her feet as the man in white tilted his hand to the side, letting the remains of the molten gun fall to the ground.

"I have never liked firearms." He stepped over the cooling

puddle of ex-pistol and toward where Nick and Lydia had retreated.

"What are you?" Nick asked, finding his voice first, even if it cracked with fear. "What the hell do you want from us?"

"My name is Lyon." He took a single step toward them, making them back away in time to his advance. "I wish for you to come with me." He paused, then spoke again thoughtfully. "Peacefully, I might add."

"Where?" Lydia asked, finally able to speak. "Go where?"

"That subject, while tempting to discuss, is, I fear, too esoteric to explore in our limited time. I may only beg your forgiveness." Lyon spoke with all the passionate delivery of a rock. But he seemed sincere, at least. The man wasn't mocking them. He took another step forward, and they took another step backward together as he approached.

When Lyon raised his hand, they both flinched as if he was going to attack them. Honestly, he might. The guy didn't seem armed, but he had melted a goddamn gun with his bare hand. Fireballs were next, for all she knew.

There was a noise from behind them, a sort of a whooshing sound and then a low hum that resembled the sound from a power generator.

Nick and Lydia turned, and for the second time, Lydia wished she hadn't.

There, painted onto the world was a black circle. Just a giant *something* made of *nothing*.

It was about eight or ten feet in diameter and seemed to hover impossibly a few inches off the ground, suspended in space. It was a blot dropped onto the surface of reality. It had no depth, no movement—just darkness.

Add it to the list.

"Please, step through the gate, if you will." Lyon was, as ridiculous as it sounded, earnestly asking them to go through it.

"You're kidding me." Lydia glanced back at him. "You're seriously joking."

"Do not force me to ask again. While I hesitate to resort to violence, my kin feel no such compulsion, I warn you. Sympathy amongst my kind is a rarity." Lyon let out a small sigh.

Lydia looked back to the inky, unmoving, and uncanny blot in space. Then, as it hadn't moved and didn't seem to be a threat, she looked back at the tall man. The monster in the suit of armor had carried a sword. This man carried nothing at all, but she felt no safer.

"What happens on the other side?" Lydia asked.

He smiled faintly with the barest twinge to thin lips. "No harm will come to you. You will continue to live. The matter is complex. Please, we may discuss this at length and leisure after you step through the gate."

She realized, looking at Lyon closer now, that he had several white markings on his face. Just like the body on the slab. It looked like a white ink tattoo, and it ran from his temple in a straight line down his cheek and to his jaw and down his neck. It was hard to see, as his skin was so pale.

"Go left?" Nick muttered to her. It meant he was going to go right. Divide and conquer—it worked last time. Maybe it'd work this time. She nodded.

It seemed their tactic wouldn't get a chance. Lyon blinked out of existence once again and reappeared standing by Nick, having closed the ten feet between them in a split second. The taller man grabbed him by the back of the hoodie and yanked him off balance. Nick screamed and fought, but there was little her friend could do. The *thing* named Lyon was too strong.

Lydia reached to try to grab Nick—or shove Lyon—but it was a useless attempt. Lyon simply backhanded her across the chest, sending her sprawling to the ground. It hadn't been a hard blow. It did nothing but sit her square on her ass. Something told her if he had wanted to crack her ribs with that hit, he could have.

Nick screamed and thrashed and struggled as hard as he could, kicking and punching at the taller man. He was in a violent, full-fledged panic.

Lyon merely reeled his arm back and threw Nick headfirst through the black hole in space. Nick screamed, but the sound broke off into silence the instant he passed through the gap. Lydia stared, stunned, and waited. Waited for anything to happen. Waited for Nick to come back out. Waited for Nick to come falling out the other side. There was only silence.

Nick was gone.

Now, it seemed like it was her turn. She realized Lyon had swiveled to face her and was walking toward her over the grass of the park.

Lydia couldn't worry about Nick anymore or she was going to be right behind him. Scrambling up to her feet, Lydia took off running in the other direction. She didn't care which way she was going. She didn't care if wound up home or in Arlington. Hell, she'd run straight to New Jersey. It didn't matter. She just needed to run away.

She made it about fifty feet to the edge of the park before rounding a corner to turn down a street. What she saw, standing in the center of the paved road, facing her down and blocking her path, sent her staggering.

On the list of recent events that were straight from a horror movie, this one was just pure madness. This was insanity. Everything else, Lydia would accept eventually after a lot of alcohol and therapy. But what was standing in the middle of the road was hopelessly unimaginable.

It was him.

The man in the suit of armor.

Edu.

He was standing there, right in the center of the road, dark and empty eye sockets turned on her. After a pause, he began walking toward her in no hurry. He was like a nightmare, walking through the dark city street.

Lydia had shot him. He was dead. She had put a bullet straight through his brain. This wasn't possible. She still had his blood on her coat.

The pointlessness suddenly hit her like a bag of bricks. They had Nick. She had cut the symbol off her arm, and it'd shown right back up on her other arm. Hopelessness struck her for the first time all day. She didn't even have a weapon anymore.

The monster in the armor finally stopped in front of her. His sword vanished from his hand, seeing that she was no threat. Lydia could only let out a small squeak of fear as he wrapped a giant, gauntleted hand around her left forearm. As he did, he squeezed down on the fresh wound on her arm. She cried out as a stabbing pain lanced up her arm when he unwittingly put pressure on her wound.

The armored man's head tilted to the side, surprised at the sound she made. He opened his hand, looking down at her forearm in his grasp. With his free hand, he pushed the fabric of her coat up to her elbow, revealing the bloody bandage on her arm.

The man sighed deeply in what *might* have been sympathy.

"Are you Edu...?" Lydia asked.

The man nodded once.

"Didn't I shoot you?"

Edu nodded again.

"Didn't I kill you?"

Another silent nod. He grasped her by her other wrist, leaving her bandaged arm alone. It seemed he didn't want to hurt her, and for that, at least, she was grateful. The man turned to stand perpendicular to her, and with his other hand gestured out in front of him in the same way Lyon had done.

Edu began to walk toward it, and her terror took over again.

Lydia tried to dig her heels in and pull back the other way, but it was like fighting the tide. He was a truck of a man, and even if he had been human, he would be far stronger than she was.

Something told her this was a one-way trip.

Edu stepped through first, and it was like watching her hand get sucked into a sawmill, with the rest of her strapped into the track. She tried desperately to fight it. Frantically, she attempted to keep her head out of that inky blackness. But the grip on her wrist hadn't lessened, and before she could even muster a scream, it overtook her.

The world was gone.

FIVE

Was she dreaming? Or was this real?

The events of the day had thrown the distinction between the two severely into question.

Lydia had no memory of getting here. She had no clue where "here" was and no idea how she wound up standing in the center of some strange, stone room. Last she knew, she had been dragged through a gate in space by a hulking man in full armor. As she turned her head, she felt strangely detached from the movement. Looking down at her arm, there was no wound there, no hastily bandaged patch of skin where she had futilely tried to remove the mark.

A dream, then. A nightmare, by the looks of things.

She was in a mausoleum.

Every surface of the walls was carved with detail that made it almost impossible to see it for what it was. Monsters and creatures tangled in a bloody feast among stone vines that seemed to wind around each other with no rhyme or reason. Columns arched up into a vaulted ceiling filled with cryptic symbols and more of the twisted vines. Stained glass windows dominated the walls, but no light shone through them to give Lydia any clue as to what they might depict.

A winged and hooded statue stood on a dais at the head of the rectangular room, almost like an altar. Its wings were not made of feathers, but of bones, as if someone had plucked every feather from an angel. In its grasp was a bowl, in which burned several black candles.

The warm flicker of the wax tapers joined many of their peers, sitting in candelabras that dotted the eerie and solemn décor of the crypt. The room seemed built to honor one fixture in particular.

A large stone sarcophagus dominated the center of the room. Oddly enough, it had no lid. Or at least one wasn't anywhere to be found. She couldn't see into the rectangular chamber in the center to see who—or what, she amended—was lying inside.

Maybe it was empty.

Yeah, right.

Curiosity burned in her. It demanded to know what was in that coffin, what kind of monster was lying in there that was going to jump out at her. If this was like any of her other monster dreams, it was inevitable. She'd walk up, it'd jump out, she'd run away, and so on. The setting might be unique, but the setup certainly wasn't.

Curiosity got the better of her as she walked up to the enormous stone sarcophagus in the center of the room. The whole thing looked carved out of one gigantic piece of the black, smooth rock. On each of the four posts were monsters and twisting demons caught in snarling and strange poses. It was beautiful, in a nightmarish kind of way.

It looked like a style one might find in Versailles, but twisted, warped, and decidedly morbid. Whoever was in this tomb was important; she could tell that much. Or at least they thought they were and had enough money or resources to back it up.

It was a dream. This was just her mind, blasting her through a fantasy nightmare of her waking horrors. It was just another creation of her exhausted, fear-consumed brain. She had been chased by so many monsters today, it was simply making up another one.

Then why did this feel more concrete than that? More *real?* A few times in her life, Lydia had lucid dreams. They felt more like vision, being able to fly around her mind and rescript events or replay things she wanted to see again.

Stepping up onto the low single stair that raised the sarcophagus ten inches off ground level, she began to lean forward to peer into the center of the coffin. It was dark, and the shadows made it nearly impossible to see at first.

She expected a twisting mass of tentacles, or some bony, bloody creature, snarling up at her. What she saw instead, was... a man.

It was *him.*

The man in all black. Dressed as he was before, all in patterns of black-on-black-on-black. Tailored and carefully made to fit his form perfectly. The coloring made him hard to see against the obsidian coffin.

And he was still wearing that smooth, black metal mask, devoid of all features save the hole for the eye and the line that ran down from it.

The only pale skin she could see was at the barest parts of his temples, or the underside of his chin and his neck. Long black hair pooled around his head on a silk pillow.

But there was something new about him now. She hadn't seen his hands before. One in a glove—black like the rest of what he was wearing—the other clad in a metal gauntlet, looking like the claw of some great beast. It shone in the light, detailing the intricate etchings that ran over the surface. The tips of the fingers ended in wicked, painfully sharp-looking claws.

It took her a long moment to realize his chest was rising and falling a slow, deep pattern. This man wasn't dead—he was asleep.

Lydia swallowed thickly.

She should run.

She should turn and run.

This man was obviously not someone to be tangled with. He was a monster, lying in repose, ready to strike. Lydia knew it. But something about him made her unable to look away. Made her too curious to bolt, somehow drawn in by him.

Lydia was dreaming, she reminded herself. This was only a nightmare. Just the convoluted mess of her subconscious mind, summoning up the bizarre man in in black.

It was that false sense of safety that led her to reach her hand slowly down to touch his smooth metal mask.

She should have known better.

Just before her fingers touched the surface, the clawed hand snapped around her wrist. It clamped down around her like a steel trap.

Lydia screamed.

* * *

How did you find me here, little one?

Curious. Utterly curious. The mystery of Lydia seemed destined to continue unabated. Now, he found her lurking within *his* mind. A shadow of her dreaming self had manifested within his tomb.

He sensed no power in her, save for the call of the mark she wore on her arm. Those chosen by the Ancients called to Aon and all his ilk like the scent of a fox might do a hound on a hunt. They were drawn to them—

hungered for them—wished to take them as the prey they were.

She drew close to him, the look on her face of pure fear. But there was something else that burned in her eyes—something he witnessed when she saw him standing in the hallway of her dreary place of employment.

Curiosity.

Fascination.

The strength to stare at the monster and find, perhaps, something intriguing in its horror.

He remained still. He wished to see what she might do. She was not the only one finding themselves rapt by the strangeness of the moment.

He had his answer as she reached out to touch him. To place timid fingertips against his metal mask. Not to remove it, but seemingly drawn to it. To him.

Although was *almost* tempted to see how far this would go —his mind flashing to thoughts of making violent love to her in his own sarcophagus nearly forcing him to laugh and ruin the game—there was one problem.

No one dared to touch him.

No one.

His hand snapped around her wrist as she drew too close. She screamed, and he laughed at the beautiful sound.

* * *

Light reflecting off a glass cylinder filled with bubbling liquid was the first thing Lydia became aware of. The movement was fascinating—the constant, repetitive rise of bubbles drifting upward before disappearing.

It all felt like a dream. Even more so than wherever Lydia just was a second ago. It was easy to believe that was true, looking at that tube of glass with the bubbling liquid. Why was it she felt like she was in some sort of medical lab? What was it about the smell in her nose that reminded her of a hospital?

Lydia remembered a hole in space. Maybe she had been hallucinating that and the rest of her awful day. Maybe she had a brain tumor or scarlet fever. Really, which way would she rather have it? That this was real, or fake?

The sharp smell in the air reminded her of sterilizers and rubbing alcohol. The scent woke her up. She must have passed out again the moment she had closed her eyes.

"Ah. Good evening." It was a voice she didn't recognize. It took a long time for her to manage to lift her head and even longer to realize what it was she was looking at.

The man in front of her looked like a nightmare straight out of one of her favorite movies. He was wearing a mask, but not a normal medical or surgical mask. This one looked more like something you'd wear to a masquerade ball. It covered maybe the top thirty percent of his face, covering one eye down to his cheekbone, then crossing up over the bridge of his nose and then up to his hairline, leaving his other eye exposed. There was nothing visible through the single eye hole of the mask, which seemed to be the trend. The surface of the mask was a dark purple matte painted finish, with more of those strange symbols and writing, etched in black.

The one eye she could see was a sharp and unnatural yellow. What she could see of his face was handsome, but austere. Aloof and unapproachable. Thin lips were pressed into the expression of a man who was wondering exactly how hard she was about to make his life.

He wore a white linen smock, and it was spattered with liquids of various colors. Luckily, none of it looked like fresh blood. For the moment, anyway. Anything was fair game at this point. But that, sadly, was not the worst of it. The man, nightmarish as he might be, wasn't what was making the recently recurring and familiar feeling of terror rise in her chest.

Lydia was strapped to a table.

The top half of the platform she was on was ratcheted to pivot upward. Leather straps held her legs down, and another one was tied around her ribcage. Her right arm had a cuff around the wrist. The belts, dark brown and untreated leather, were pulled tight around her.

Lydia's left arm was strapped to a leather upholstered platform that kept it lifted and off to the side. It seemed her forearm was the focus of attention. A leather belt was tied around her wrist and her elbow, holding it lashed firmly to the removable armrest. The whole table looked like an assembly from the late nineteenth century.

Her bandages were removed, and the man was standing next to her, hunched slightly over her arm as if he had been in the middle of something.

The strange fuzzy feeling in her mind fled and was quickly replaced with adrenaline. Lydia thrashed against the straps. "Let me go!"

"I suppose you were right," a woman said from her other side. "I concede that the ties are indeed necessary."

The man sighed and reached toward a table that was out of her direct field of view. When his hand returned in front of her, he was holding a syringe. Just like the table, it was horribly dated looking, a metal case around a glass container, with two large circles for his fingers.

"No!" Lydia froze. "No, stop!" she shouted. "Please, don't," she begged the man. "I—I'll stop struggling. Please. Just don't."

The man paused and eyed Lydia scrupulously, arching one dubious eyebrow. "If you continue to fuss, I have no qualms about rendering you unconscious. It matters not to me either way."

It felt safer to be awake, even if she was helpless. "I'll behave. I promise."

"For now." It was clear he didn't believe her.

"Darling..." the woman cajoled him.

Lydia didn't dare glance away from the man looming over her arm with a syringe loaded with God knew what to see who —or what—else was in the room.

The man sighed. "Very well." He put the syringe back down on the metal table with a clink.

Lydia let out the breath she had been holding and watched as the man eyed her warily. He looked as though he expected Lydia to begin thrashing around again at any moment. It wasn't that she wasn't tempted. But it was clear it would take her far longer to get loose of the straps he was using to tie her down than it would for him to knock her out.

Besides, something felt weird. Off. Detached and out of sync again. Like Lydia's head was stuffed with cotton, or as though she were a little drunk. It felt like laughing gas at the dentist. "Did you drug me?" She was both offended and curious all at the same time.

"Of course. I cannot have you bashing about while I work. And I assumed," he paused as he pointedly cast a glance off somewhere else into the room, "correctly so, that you would be terrified of where you now find yourself." Lydia realized the man had a vaguely British accent. He was human—or at least had been at one point. His yellow-colored eye put his current status up for debate.

"I think I have a good reason to be terrified." It was hard not to be annoyed at the situation.

"Perhaps. But, that notwithstanding, I have a task to perform. I ask that you do your best to keep still." He went to fiddling with something on the table next to him, pulling something out of a container and wiping it down.

"Are you going to hurt me?"

"If I were planning such, I hardly would care if you struggled. As the case may be, I am attempting to avoid causing you undue injury. Now." He glanced at her with a vaguely beleaguered expression, "If I may have a moment's peace?"

"Buddy, don't get huffy with me like I'm inconveniencing you." Lydia didn't quite know where she got the nerve to be so spunky with him. Maybe it was the drugs he had given her. "I was abducted by monsters. and I'm strapped to a fucking table. Sorry for taking up your precious *fucking* time."

The woman laughed from the other side of the room. "Oh, Maverick. The young lady has your number already, I see."

The man—Maverick—sighed and turned to his table. He was mixing things together from various jars into what looked like salve. "Pardon me for wishing to be allowed a moment to focus before I go to work."

"Yes, yes, no one appreciates your plight." The woman, whoever she was, clearly loved to tease Maverick. And might also love him in general, judging by the affection in her tone.

Lydia turned to find the source, but they were standing behind her. She was in a laboratory of some kind. A nice one, even if it had more business being a printed illustration in a history textbook than in the real world. Two walls of the room were dominated by bookcases, and several of the shelves were taken over not by books, but with brass gadgetry and jars with contents she couldn't make sense of. It looked like a laboratory from the nineteenth century, somewhere in one of Harvard's older buildings. Everything was cast in warm tones of wood, brass, copper, and glowing amber light.

What the hell was happening to her? She kept snapping back to that every few seconds as she realized she had no idea where she was, who was sitting there next to her, and no sense of what was actually going on. Or why she was here. Or—wait.

"Hold up. What work?" She finally caught up with what he had said. Maverick had said "before going to work." Man, that had taken her a really, really long time. The drugs he had given her must have been something pretty damn strong.

"I am attempting to repair that which someone decided was a prudent course of action." The man was focusing on her arm. His tone was still empty, and yet somehow judgmental in his certainty. "Although the butcher appears to have had more experience working with a pig's carcass than a living body."

"Hey!" Lydia bristled at the insult.

Maverick looked up at her. A brown eyebrow—the visible one—raised slightly in surprise. "You did this to yourself?"

"Yeah." She did her best to glare at him. Damn, those drugs were good. She should be screaming her head off, but instead, she was getting defensive. "And I'm a leftie, so I was using my off hand, so step off, buddy."

"Hm," was his reply. He looked back down to Lydia's arm and resumed whatever he had been doing before she woke up, which appeared to be picking gauze out of the wound, one stray piece of cotton at a time. The bits of string pulled on her skin as her body had tried to heal around the offending items.

That should have hurt. Yanking the little cotton cords out of her skin should have at least stung. Lydia realized she couldn't feel her arm. Not at all. She wiggled her fingers and was happy at least she had control of it. But what he was doing should have felt like something. Maverick must have used local anesthetic or something of the kind. But what kind of local anesthetic worked like that, she had no clue.

"You must forgive him," the woman said again. She also had an accent. Lydia couldn't quite place it, but it sounded almost Eastern European. "That is his reaction when he is mildly impressed."

The woman finally walked to where Lydia could see her. She had long brown hair in a careful braid coiled at the base of her neck. She wore a dress that looked like it dated to somewhere in the eighteenth century if it had gone to a fetish convention along the way. Straps and strange archaic appliqués were added on top of a complicated, corseted dress with many layers.

She also wore a mask. This one covered the entire right side of her face, save for her jawline, leaving her whole mouth exposed. Her lips were full and painted a deep purple to match her mask which offset the deep gray tones of her dress. Purple was apparently the motif with these two.

"Did I interrupt you two on the way to a masquerade ball?" The thought immediately came to Lydia's mind.

The woman's features bloomed into a broader smile, it was a warm and kind expression. "I am afraid not."

"Where am I? Who are you people? What the hell is happening?" Lydia launched the questions in the order they came to her. Stupid drugs.

The woman laughed. It wasn't a cruel laugh, but it was as sympathetic as her expression. "Oh, my dear, I am sorry. This must all be so much to take in."

"That isn't an answer to literally anything I asked." She took a breath to try to think through the drugs, but they were really clouding her mind. "Is Nick okay?"

"Who?" The woman blinked.

"The guy who came here with me."

"I am sure he is fine and with the others," Maverick muttered, clearly focused on his task. "We do not harm those we take, contrary to your current belief."

"Oh," was all Lydia could muster. "He's my friend. I'm just worried about him."

"That is commendable, but I assure you, he is well," the woman interjected for Maverick.

Lydia had a million questions. "Where'd the big guy go?" She turned to look around the room to see if she had missed anyone else looming in a corner. Like, y'know, a man in a suit of armor the size of a small tank. Or a scary man in black with a clawed gauntlet on one hand.

The odd woman walked up to stand close to Lydia's other side, so she didn't need to twist her head around to look at her. "I am Aria. The gentleman with the poor bedside manners is my husband, Maverick. Lord Edu deposited you into our care when he realized you were injured."

"I do not have poor bedside manners." Maverick raised his head slightly from where he was still hunched over her arm. "I am merely focusing on the task at hand. It has been some time since I have had to play nursemaid, might I remind you."

"Oh, great, you're a jerk *and* you're out of practice? That's fantastic!" Probably a bad call to insult the guy cleaning her wound, but she didn't exactly care. "What the hell is going on?"

Panic rose in her chest again as everything came crashing back all at once, every bit of fear and confusion buzzing up like a swarm of angry bees. Each thought riled up the next until they were swirling around each other in a self-perpetuating cycle.

"Calm yourself." Aria placed her hand on Lydia's shoulder. "We mean you no harm. You are safe here. Lord Edu was concerned you may scar or become infected. He wished us to tend to your wound to ensure otherwise."

Deep breath. Whatever was going on, panic wouldn't help. Lydia tried to repeat her mantra from her EMT days. *Panic later. Deal with this first. Panic later.*

Lydia rested her head back against the reclined surface of the table, let out a sigh, and ran through the realization once more to try and solidify it, to try to get it through her own dense, panic-stricken mind. Aria was right; neither of them were hurting her. In fact, Maverick had numbed her arm. The only damage she had on her person was what she had done to herself, and he was trying to fix it.

Hell, from what she could gather, the only reason she was strapped to the table was to keep her from panicking and struggling. "I'm sorry. I just don't know what's going on. In one day, I woke up with a tattoo I didn't get, I've been attacked and chased and abducted. And waking up here, like this, is not okay."

"I know," Aria said consolingly and ran her hand along Lydia's shoulder, petting her like she might a family member. There was an odd, sincere sympathy there. "There is much to understand all at once. There is nothing to apologize for."

Lydia turned her attention to Maverick. "Sorry for calling you a jerk."

He only grunted quietly in reply as he took some salve out of a jar and wiped it on the exposed wound with a swab. The circular incision she had made in her arm looked like a bad third-degree burn at this point. Lydia couldn't help but watch, fascinated, the drug in her system still making everything seem slightly out of sync and fluffy. "It will not need stitches."

Good talk, buddy. She looked back over at Aria. "Can you please answer some of my questions?" Maybe she could try again, this time with a more polite and less panicky approach.

"It is not that I do not wish to tell you, but I do not know how best to explain it all without causing you more undue worry." She looked almost embarrassed. "Soon, you will be back in the care of the Priest. Talk to him. He has far more... experience in these matters than me."

"The Priest?" Lydia asked.

"You met him, I believe. Lord Edu brought him to Earth to help retrieve you and your friend. His name is Lyon, although we all tend to refer to him as the Priest, somewhat pejoratively, I am afraid." Aria smiled down at her. "Lord Edu believed a more considerate approach may succeed where he had failed." Aria leaned in slightly and lowered her voice—as if someone might hear. "Did you truly kill Lord Edu?"

"Well, it obviously didn't stick." Lydia felt like she was missing something major. "I swear I did, though." A hundred thoughts and questions tried to pile out of her mind all at once and got stuck in the door jamb of her brain and couldn't get anywhere useful. Finally, one of them managed to squeeze out of the crowd with a pop. "You said Edu brought him to Earth. That means I'm no longer on Earth...?"

Aria sighed sadly and looked over at Maverick, who glanced up from his work with a scolding expression of *I told you so.* Aria gritted her teeth for a moment before looking down at her. She was quite beautiful, even with the eerie mask.

"No, my dear." Her expression was of a woman who wondered if she had just hit the detonate button on the armed bomb. "This is not Earth."

Lydia could scream—could panic, fight, thrash—beg for freedom, throw up or cry. Maybe it was the drugs, or she was just exhausted and tired of being afraid. But something in her fell flat at the news and gave up trying to condone and understand everything that she had seen and heard so far.

This wasn't Earth anymore.

Really, she had no reason to doubt them after everything she'd been through. No reason to think the strange and flat hole through space she had witnessed wasn't actually just that. A gate to another place. It felt so ludicrous, she almost wanted to laugh, but she was too tired to even muster that.

Instead, she stared up at the ceiling. It had a beautiful chandelier up there, with lights upon winding brass arms, burning to resemble candles. The classical fixture was attached into a ceiling medallion whose curling acanthus leaves looked twisted and warped. Too pointed and angular—like the writing on her arm. Like the writing on their masks.

"I want to go home." It felt childish. She felt childish.

"I promise you, in a few days, if not shorter, this will be your home. You will be at peace with all that has happened. You will see this world as a new opportunity. I vow it," Aria pledged to her adamantly.

"A point of advice." Maverick gestured at the wound in her arm with the back end of a swab. "Living tissue does not separate like dead tissue. It is clear to me that is with what you are accustomed to working. The dead skin comes away from the matter underneath quite cleanly." Talk about a change of subject. The man had the air of a professor, and suddenly she felt like she was back in med school. "What you see here, the blistering of the dermis, is due to the trauma you caused when you, as far as I can tell, *ripped* your own skin off."

"Look." It was silly to get defensive at his judgmental tone, but it was easy. Everything else was too big, too insane. But arguing with a man and explaining to him exactly how impressive her home surgery really was, considering the circumstances, was easy. "I did the best I could with what I had."

"Which was what, precisely?" There was the arch to the brown eyebrow again.

"My hobby knife and a pair of forceps. And that's it. And yes, fine, I work on dead people. I'm a forensic autopsy tech. What do you want from me?" That really was the motto of the past day.

"Hm." There was that mildly impressed noise Aria had pointed out to her earlier. "That must have been immensely painful."

Lydia laughed at the understatement. "Yeah. I woke up on my floor."

Maverick shook his head, but there was a faint smile on his features. His one visible yellow eye was looking at her somewhat bemused, if still somehow also managing to look like a college professor. "Well, as you can see," he gestured to her other arm, where the small backward N with the swirl had reappeared, "the effort was sadly wasted."

"I had to try."

"You are not the first." Maverick shrugged. "I do not recommend trying again."

"Noted." Lydia let out a breath and rested her head against the table again. "Good job changing the subject."

"It is a gift," came his dry reply.

Lydia had to laugh again. If that was his attempt at a joke, she didn't honestly know, but she found it funny. Then again, Lydia found humor in the worst of things. She worked in a morgue, after all.

"Goodness me, Maverick. Note the calendar, for someone has finally arrived who understands your humor." Aria had taken her hand off Lydia's shoulder at some point—and she hadn't noticed, damn drugs—and had wandered over to a bookcase to start leafing through books.

"It was not a jest." Maverick's response was deadpan as he began to wrap up the wound on her arm. "I will inform Lord Edu you are ready to join the others." He picked up the syringe on the table, the one he had threatened her with earlier.

Lydia tensed reflexively. "Wait, wait! I'm not struggling."

"No, but you certainly will be in short order. It is better for you to be transported in an unconscious state." Maverick swabbed a spot on her arm and inserted the needle with no other pomp or circumstance. "I will not have you thrashing about and tearing off the bandage, or worse, re-injuring yourself." He depressed the plunger.

It was astonishing how quickly blood circulated in the body. All through med school, Lydia had been impressed with how fast something could go from point A to point B in the bloodstream. And this moment was no exception.

The world began to dim.

Oh. Oh, hell, please, no... *not again.*

* * *

"Master Edu wonders why you did not simply leave her unconscious the entire time," Ylena said from Edu's side. Her flowing red dress made a faint whisper on the wood floor as she moved to stand beside him.

Edu looked down at the young woman on the table, the straps that held her there undone. The human girl was lying senseless to the world, her eyes shut, head rolled to one side. Her blonde hair was splayed around her face, falling in soft curls along what he decided were sultry and beautiful features.

Edu was not one to hesitate in appreciating the beauty of those around him. But it was not her appearance that had struck an ember of curiosity in him, for he was privileged to enjoy the company of any he saw fit to have.

Beauty alone did not inspire such attention as he now paid this young one—coming to fetch her from the doctor in person, as it were.

It was that she had, quite simply, caught him off guard.

The look of defiance in her flashing blue eyes as she had fired off her weapon into his head had been breathtaking. Firearms had evolved significantly over the past hundred and eighty-odd years since he had walked Earth. He had not expected so much impact out of the little pop-toy.

The woman was undoubtedly of stronger will than most he had met in his many, many years, and she was amusing to chase, however briefly the pursuit had lasted. Edu had underestimated her strength of character when hunting her, and that misjudgment had allowed her to kill him.

He had not died once in a very long time, and it was with no small amount of chagrin that he had awoken from the injury she had paid him.

"For the same reason I suspect you come in person to fetch her." Maverick stood from his desk and was wiping his hands off on a damp cloth. The man was shorter than Edu by a fair length, but then again, most creatures who once claimed humanity found themselves in such a state. "Curiosity. Aria wished to cast a glance into the modern mind before the woman is to be added to our ranks."

Ah, yes. The Fall was a cause for much trouble in his world.

It upended the balance of things, adding new life and new invigoration into a dead and dying world. Like fish, scrambling for new territory when more were added to a tank, it was a cause for nervousness and excitement.

"Master Edu thanks you for your service." Ylena bowed her head.

No, in fact, he had not done any such thing. He admonished Ylena silently, and her psychic connection with him would allow her to feel it as certainly as the moons might rise. Her expression did not change, and he knew she did not care for his scolding. *"Do not speak for me, Ylena."*

Ylena was often wont to soften Edu's manners. To add a sense of civility where he had none, she would usually tell him. *"That is all I do."* Her voice in his head was as familiar as his own.

"It is an honor, of course." Maverick bowed his head.

Platitudes and niceties. This was what Edu hated above all else. He despised such bending and scraping. Maverick no more respected Edu than he did a table lamp, and his disdain was as clear as the Earthen sun. But the doctor rightly feared him.

He had the sudden overwhelming urge to grasp Maverick by the back of the head and ram his skull through the wall. He could. He was a king.

Edu felt his hand twitch.

Ylena's presence entered his mind once more. *"Please do not entertain this desire further. He has done nothing to deserve your wrath."*

Edu was not keen on self-restraint. Yet in this case, the moment of indulgence would cost him more trouble and annoyance in short order. Maverick was regent and elder of the House of Words. Sighing from under his mask, he let the urge pass.

Very well.

Leaning down, he picked the young woman up in his arms.

She was a tiny thing, with curves in all the right places. She had full lips, and he wondered what it might be like to touch them. But he was in no rush. He could have her when he wished. There would be many amusing creatures worth exploring in the years to follow, and for that reason alone, Edu always looked forward to when their worlds aligned.

Perhaps he would bid her to his chambers for a night or two, once the ceremony had come and gone. Playing with someone so willful and with such conviction would be entertaining, with her flashing blue eyes and fiery spirit. He suspected she would be easy to take but harder to tame. All the better. But that was for another time. For now, the girl must go back with the others.

And await her turn for the Fall.

SIX

It was like helplessly re-watching a film where someone dies. No amount of knowing what was going to happen would help the poor, doomed character on the screen. No amount of yelling at the TV would change the outcome. It was scripted. It was unavoidable.

But *why* was she stuck watching it again?

She was back in the crypt where that man in black had been sleeping. "I fucking hate this." Putting her head in her hands she let out a wavering sigh. This was stupid. Abjectly stupid. She wanted to go home. She wanted to wake up. She wanted this to all be the result of her having accidentally taken some serious drugs and having a really, really bad trip.

It seemed like life was really out to kick her in the teeth, though. Because instead of waking up in bed, or even in a hospital, here she was—yet again trapped in a creepy-ass tomb with some creepy-ass dude.

"Fine! Fine. Let's get this over with." She threw up her hands in frustration and walked toward the edge of that obsidian sarcophagus. Taking a breath, she stepped up onto the lip and peered over, bracing herself to see him there.

But he was nowhere to be seen.

Her shoulders fell. "Oh, no."

A hand twisted in her hair, and a presence at her back pressed her to the edge of the stone sarcophagus, trapping her there. A voice that sounded like a knife wrapped in black velvet purred into her ear. "Well, hello..."

She did the only logical thing.

She tried to elbow him as hard as she could. But the moment she reeled up for the attack, he grabbed her wrist with his other hand and used it to pin both her arms to her chest. His arm was wrapped around her, and she was struck by the smell of dust, old books, and expensive cologne.

"Let me *go!*" She bit the words out between clenched teeth. Dream or not, this was bullshit.

The man—the thing—behind her chuckled. The sound sent a shiver up her spine. "And where are your manners?"

"You have got to be kidding me, you—"

The hand in her hair tightened. "Careful, little one."

Maverick hadn't been out to hurt her. Hell, even the walking tank named Edu's reaction to her wound seemed like he didn't want her to be in pain.

But this guy? This guy, all bets were off.

She swallowed her insult. And her pride. She didn't know what she was up against. "Please."

"Good." He released her before retreating a few steps away. She whirled, not wanting to keep her back turned to him for any longer than she had to. He stretched his arms out to his sides as if to pretend he was harmless—she wasn't buying it.

She could see now the stray few gray hairs serving as the only contrast of color in his long, jet-black hair. He was taller than average but not nearly as much as Lyon, nor was he nearly as broad as Edu. But he was just as intimidating. His appearance seemed cultivated for that purpose.

The man's very dated, if expensive-looking, three-piece suit was tailored to accent an angular but toned build. He looked like a living nightmare. Maybe he was.

"Who are you?" She gripped the edge of the sarcophagus, fighting the urge to just run out the door. She was in a dream, there was no telling that what was out there wasn't worse. Besides, she figured it was like a coyote—if she ran, he'd chase.

"We will get to that, in due time." He hummed thoughtfully. "I am more intrigued by answering the question of just *how* it seems you and I have been introduced."

"You—don't know?"

"No." He pulled in a sharp breath through his nose and let it out in a small sigh as if conceding a debate in his mind. "Ah, well. You will discover this soon enough. I fear my grasp on my own mind may be a bit... tenuous at best."

"Oh, good. I've dreamed up an insane nightmare man." She ran a hand over her face.

"You believe I am a figment of your mind? How charming." He chuckled. "No, my dear. I am very real. My shattered mind may play tricks upon me, but of that fact, I am certain. You merely have found yourself inside my sleeping psyche. Or, perhaps, I have found myself attached to yours. I have been seeing quite a lot of you lately."

"What does that mean?"

"You really must tidy your kitchen. Although, you will never see it again. I suppose now it hardly matters." He shrugged dismissively. "And why own houseplants if you seemingly never water them?"

Her eyes went wide. "You were really there? When—when I saw you in the hallway?"

"Yes. Terrible artwork. Who puts watercolor paintings on the walls in a morgue?" He huffed. "Truly. What is the modern phrase you lot seem to enjoy? 'Lipstick on a pig?'"

She was stuck in a nightmare listening to a nightmare man critique her office's choice of wall decor. Lacing her hands into her hair, she gripped the strands, trying to use the tension against her scalp to help her think. "What the hell is going on?"

"Not Hell, my dear. Under. And you will find out soon enough." He pondered her for a moment, his head tilting just slightly to the side, similarly to Edu, if not as pronounced. "Though why we have found ourselves in this predicament, I can barely guess. I can only hope..." he paused as he took a step back toward her. She froze, every muscle in her body tensing as he approached her.

She should run.

She should really, really run.

But if she did, she knew he'd make things *far* worse for her.

So, she stayed locked in place as he closed the distance between them.

His hands rested on either side of hers on the edge of the sarcophagus as he leaned in close to finish his sentence. "... that you are bound to join me." The dark rumble of his words sent her stomach twisting into strange knots. Terror, yes. But now something else joined it.

"J—join you—where? Here?"

"As entertaining as it would be, no. This place is merely where I reside during my... forced absence from the throne. All will be made clear in time." The man lifted his clawed gauntlet from her wrist and hovered the points of his knife-like fingers over her cheek.

"Wait, please—"

"Once more, you ask for my restraint?" It was clear he was deeply amused. He curled his clawed fingers into his palm and ran the metal knuckle down her cheek instead. It was a tender, gentle gesture. But it terrified her all the same. "How lovely. But know this, my dear—begging for my mercy is a wasted effort, though I do *adore* the sound of it. Do continue. Just know that it will be fruitless."

She was shaking like a leaf. "What do you want from me?"

"We shall see, in time. But for now, if you do not wish to be here, then simply wake. I am not trapping you in this place." He shrugged again, idly.

"I—I can't." Lydia had never stammered so much in her life. "He drugged me. Maverick."

"Hm. Yes. I saw." The man let out a deep and beleaguered sigh. He hung his head and shook it, the dark tendrils of his hair falling alongside the black of his mask. The only difference between the two was how they reflected the flickering candle-light. "That man, for all his intelligence, is an utter moron."

"You know him?"

"I very well should. I am the one who brought Maverick to Under. I knew him as a mortal man before he came through the gate and Fell to the House of Words and became its regent." Somehow, he managed to sound oddly conversational, even as he was looming over her like a creature out of a slasher film.

"House of Words?"

"You would not understand. Once you Fall, all will be made clear."

"Fall where?"

The man sighed wistfully. "The uninitiated are always so wonderfully naïve. Did you tell Maverick of our previous encounters? I was not watching the entire time, I admit." He rested his metal palm against her jawline, the dagger-like blade of his thumb running across her cheek. It made her shiver, and she pressed harder against the edge of the sarcophagus. The touch sent her heart lodging into her throat.

"No—I thought you were a nightmare." She swallowed her heart back down. "I'm still not totally sure you aren't."

The man leaned in insistently. "You must not tell anyone that we have spoken. Do not speak a word that you know anything of me. Do not mention anything of me."

"What will happen if I do?"

"It will mean your life, little one. They will kill you in a heartbeat, the Fall be damned, if they learn that I have drawn us —even unwittingly—together."

"But why?" Lydia swallowed thickly.

The man ignored her question as he finally removed his clawed hand from her. "You wish to wake up, do you not?"

"Yeah?"

"But you are drugged and cannot do so on your own."

"I don't think so?" Why was this conversation suddenly making her very nervous?

"I suspect I know how to force the matter."

"What do you mean?"

"Well, Lydia," he purred out her name, and it made her skin flood with goosebumps, "it is a distinct pleasure to meet you. My name is Aon, and you will come to fear me."

Before she could react, he drove the fingers of his clawed gauntlet deep into her ribcage.

* * *

Aon could not help but laugh.

Twice now? *Twice* she came to his crypt?

He could not be solely to blame for this series of charming little interludes between them.

This time, he had sensed her on the edges of his mind, sneaking into his dreams like a thief through a window. This time, he was not caught nearly so off-guard. How delighted he had been as he had watched from the shadows as she crept toward his sarcophagus in the center of the mausoleum.

While she may not have caught him by surprise, his own sudden hunger for her, did. He felt it surge in him like a wolf on the hunt. He wanted to see her look at him in terror. He wanted to feel her body against his. Wondered what she might smell like.

This reaction to her presence was not a common occur-
rence for him.

It was not that he did not have such physical urges. He did.
He certainly did. Just as much, if not more so, than any of the
others. He just simply did not find the need to pay such things
any mind. He had the self-restraint to not entertain himself in
such a way as he was tempted to do now, with this little curious
mortal who had blundered into his mind.

Not to mention—no one dared let him eke out his desires
upon them.

Not for long, anyway.

The sadist. The madman. The revolting demon. The
mastermind and manipulator.

The only company who sought him out were the curious or
the power-hungry. The ones who wondered how nightmarish a
night with him truly was—or those who wished to secure a
position of favor with the King of Shadows. He never kept
them around for more than an evening or two. Either he
became bored of their political games, or they came to realize
that the cost of such favor from the King of Shadows was far
too high.

The core of the matter was always thus—they despised him.
He made them pay for it in flesh.

He had earned his reputation.

And he enjoyed it.

But this little thing? This mortal, who gazed at him in such
terrified fascination?

She carried no hatred for him. No innate disgust. She
would, soon enough. But for now, she was free of the corrup-
tion of the Ancients.

He could have *fun* with this one.

And she was simply far too tempting.

How warm she had felt against him. How perfectly her
shape had nestled against his. How deeply he had wished to

press harder forward, to hear her gasp, to *take her* in their dreams. Damn him to the pits, he wanted her.

The best games are played with patience, you old fool. He had refrained. Besides, there was another matter to consider. Soon, she would Fall and become of Under. And the moment she was adorned with the true marks of their kind, their game would be over.

What was the point, then?

A useless foray in a dream?

No. In a days' time, she would look at him with the same disdain and disgust as all the others. Even those who fell to his own house found him unsettling at best—abhorrent at worst. They served him out of their desire to stay alive, not out of any sense of *loyalty*.

And there was another issue that he knew would supersede any desire Aon held for the mortal.

Edu.

Hate boiled in him at the mere thought of the King of Flames. Aon had seen how Edu had lifted Lydia in his arms. The gentleness in the way he carried her. Edu would have his own designs upon her, certainly, for having bested him in the hunt.

Although, the mute bastard had desires upon nearly *everyone* and *everything*. Where Aon prided himself on his discerning palate, Edu had the refinement of a goat—devouring anything he could reach. *Disgusting.*

Usually, Aon could not care less for those Edu chose to bed. He was not one to quibble over the distribution of garbage, after all. But Lydia had sparked in him something quite uncommon.

It had not been just fear he saw in those shining blue eyes of hers. Oh, may the pits preserve him. There was still curiosity burning there. *Excitement.*

Hidden and perhaps mistakable by anyone who was not so

perfectly and personally acquainted with the spectrum of terror as he was. Oh, she was afraid of him. That was for certain. But even as she had recoiled from him in terror, he saw the glint in her eyes. She was fascinated by him, even as she was trembling in fear.

I could find another reason to make you tremble.

And when he had approached her? She had stood there, locked, looking up at his visage with that intoxicating mix of fear and nervous delight. He would savor that expression until the end of his days. So rarely had he ever been the recipient of so perfect a thing as that.

And when he had touched her cheek? Her cheeks went pink in a blush as he trailed the tips of his knife-like fingers over her tender skin. *Oh, be still my black heart.* It had taken all his willpower to control the *rest* of him, lest he give her a new reason to be understandably alarmed. She was not ready. The flicker of desire was there, but it was not yet burning.

He was many things, but he was not a brute. He wished for a *willing* partner. There was far more joy to be had luring her into the shadows with him.

Like all things, their time had drawn to a close. And he woke her up the best way he knew how—violence. He had driven the daggers of his claws deep into her ribcage. The shock of it had instantly shattered the moment.

I will see you soon, Lydia. One way or another.

It was time to wake up. He had work to do.

* * *

Lydia woke with a jolt, her heart pounding in her ears. Her stomach swirled dangerously as everything moved around her. "Oh, damn it." She guessed a nightmare shouldn't be unexpected, given recent events. But that felt so damn *real*.

And whoever that guy was, he was a piece of work. The

feeling of his clawed hand digging into her ribs lingered in her mind and made her shudder. If he was real, she knew she was in trouble. If he was fake, she needed therapy.

"Jesus Christ," came a familiar voice next to her. "You had me scared."

When the world finally managed to sit still long enough that she could uncover her eyes without throwing up, she blinked the world into focus. Someone was kneeling next to her and blotting out whatever dim light was around them. "Nick?"

"God, Lyd, you were freaking out, and I couldn't wake you up."

As she sat up, he put a hand on her back to help. The world was still threatening to spin out from around her at any point, so she took her time. She threw her arms around him, and he returned the gesture. After a long moment of silent relief, she pushed away from him to try to survey where they were.

Lydia was sitting on the ground with Nick kneeling next to her. The terrain in question was rough, uncarved rock, dark and covered in pebbles and stones. A cave. It was lit by torches that were shoved into metal rings hammered into the cavernous walls. The fire cast flickering and conflicting shadows across the floor of the stone surfaces.

They weren't alone. There were *dozens* of people in the cave with them, maybe a hundred, scattered about and sitting or standing on the uneven surfaces. Some were leaning against the walls, and she saw one person lying on the ground with a coat shoved under his head, trying to sleep. Everyone was dressed in various garbs from what seemed like multiple seasons—some in winter coats, some in summer gear—all mixes of races, colors, genders, and ages. No children, though. She noticed that reasonably quickly. Everyone here was an adult.

There was a quiet murmur of conversation, and she couldn't really pick up on any of it, except that a lot of it wasn't in English. "Who are these people? Where are we?"

"As far as I can tell, they were taken like us. They all have marks. As to where? Fuck if I know." Nick let out a low breath and ran his hand over his short, scruffy brown hair, ruffling it. He did that when he was nervous or scared. The look on his face was that of a man who was one good startle away from losing his mind. "When that tall asshole threw me through the hole, I wound up here, sprawled out on the rocks. Same with everyone else."

"How long have you been here?" Lydia tried to focus on the mystery. The other option was a panic attack.

"About four hours." He paused. "What happened to you? You got carried in by that giant freak in the armor twenty minutes ago. Didn't you say you shot him?"

"I did. I don't know how he's still alive. He caught me a minute after Lyon got you. I didn't even make it down the block."

"Then where've you been?"

"I don't know that either. I woke up in a weird medical lab out of some antique textbook. There was a guy named Maverick and his wife, Aria. They were wearing freaky masks and looked like they weren't... they weren't normal. He patched up my arm."

"What do you mean, patched up?"

Lydia rolled up her coat sleeve, and sure enough, there was the small square of gauze, taped professionally to her arm. No blood spots had oozed through, and it shockingly didn't hurt. She poked it curiously and still, nothing. She could feel sensation from it, but no pain. Whatever Maverick had put on it had helped.

"They didn't torture you? Didn't grill you for information?"

"He was just doing what he was told. Then I guess the guy in the armor—Edu—came to get me and brought me back here. I was out cold by that point again. Assholes drugged me up."

"Huh," was all he had to say.

"Nobody's hurt you?" she asked Nick.

"Nobody's said anything to us at all." Nick stood from the ground and brushed the gravel and bits of dirt from his jeans. He reached out a hand to her to help her stand. Finally getting up to her feet, she wobbled for a moment but managed to stay upright. *Fuckin' drugs.*

The cave was about fifty by eighty feet, give or take. A large wooden double door with iron rings on it, like you'd find in a medieval castle, looked to be the only way in or out. She pointed at them. "Has anybody tried those to see if that's locked?"

"Well?" Nick blinked. "No, honestly. We're all pretty scared. The monsters you and I've met have been, uh, human-looking. Most people were dragged here by things that weren't. I don't think anyone's looking forward to meeting what's on the other side. I've tried to talk to as many people as I could to figure out what's going on. Nobody knows anything." Nick led her away from where she had woken up and toward where a small group was sitting as he talked.

A man sitting with a young Asian woman looked up as they approached. The man was in his early forties, maybe, and had a harried look about him. The woman was cowering, her knees pulled up to her chest, her arms wrapped around them tightly in an attempt to make herself as small as possible.

"Your friend is awake." The older man smiled at her. "Hello! You must be Lydia. I am Gary." Gary stood and nearly fell over as his foot slipped on a rock. He quickly steadied himself against the wall with one hand, then extended his other hand to her. Maybe not the most coordinated man in the world, but with decent reflexes and more energy than Lydia expected. He was dressed in a button down and a pair of slacks —business casual. "Wonderful to meet you."

Lydia smiled back and shook his hand. She instantly liked the man. He had lively green eyes and friendly, if incredibly British, mannerisms. "Nice to meet you. Given the circumstances."

"Agreed, agreed." Gary sighed. "This is Kaori." Gary motioned to the Asian woman still cowering on the floor. Dark, saucer-like eyes were staring up at her in wary fear. "She does not speak much English, I'm afraid."

Lydia smiled sympathetically at her. She knew exactly how the girl felt. She was doing on the inside what Kaori was doing on the outside. "Hey, Kaori. Nice to meet you."

"You also," the girl muttered and tucked her chin into her knees. She was shaking. Poor thing.

Gary sat back down next to Kaori and put his hand on her back, trying to console her. "She's taking this all rather hard."

"I guess we all should be." Lydia turned her attention to the cave again. Some people were hunched into groups, and she heard sobbing from one corner. "None of this makes any sense."

"Nicholas told me what happened to the two of you. Very brave, trying to run. I am afraid I merely let it all happen without much fuss." Gary sighed. "I was too astonished to do much else."

Lydia had to laugh at Gary calling Nick by his full name. Nick hated that, and she saw the look on her friend's face when he couldn't quite bring himself to correct the Englishman.

"Fuck this." She'd had enough. This was stupid. They were owed explanations.

"Where're you going?" Nick asked.

"I'm trying the door."

"And if it opens?" Gary asked.

"I'm getting answers." Lydia felt a likely temporary surge of confidence and headed for the door.

"No. No, seriously, I think we should stay put. I've heard about what's been grabbing people, and what's out there... they aren't friendly." Nick quickly fell in step beside her.

"I don't care. Someone's going to tell me what's going on. And if I get eaten, fine." Did she really mean she'd be fine with being eaten? Probably not. But it sounded good when she said it. "Are you coming?"

"Yeah, okay." Nick sighed and shoved his hands into his hoodie pockets. "This is a stupid idea."

Lydia shrugged. "Door's probably locked, anyway. Come on."

Walking to the door, she picked up the large metal ring. It was roughly hammered iron, fed through a bracket that attached it to the door with heavy forged bolts. It squealed loudly as she tilted it upward. She tugged.

It swung open slowly about an inch before she stopped pulling. What kind of idiots would keep prisoners in an unlocked chamber?

Ones who know you're in a larger cage anyway.

Or worse...

Ones who plan on eating the stupid ones who leave the room.

There was a hallway on the other side, long, rocky, and lit with torches the same as the cavern they were in. The corridor twisted and turned and went on for about a hundred feet before Lydia couldn't see down it anymore as it disappeared around a bend.

The cavernous hallway was also—thankfully—empty. Nobody was standing there waiting, no monsters lurking. Not that they could see, anyway.

Who left their prisoners in an unlocked, *unguarded* cage?

"C'mon." She pulled the door open a few more inches to slip through the crack and into the hallway.

"I get the feeling we're going to get chased again." Nick sounded less than thrilled. She didn't blame him.

"Probably." He paused for a moment. "So, Kaori's cute."

"Seriously, dude?" Lydia glanced at him narrowly. "You're gonna do this now?"

"Might die soon," Nick said with a shrug. "And I just said she was cute, that's all."

Lydia shook her head and went back to focusing on the hallway that may or may not contain monsters. But that didn't stop her from whispering, "You're an asshole, Nick."

"Yup."

When they got to an intersection, she stopped. "That's... weird."

One hallway met the other and just seemed to melt out of stone and into a carved, finished area. As soon as the cavern touched the intersection of hallways, it became a polished marble. But what was really peculiar about it was it didn't look like the stone hallway had been carved out of the cave.

It looked more like the cavern was trying to eat the building. Like lava flow, oozing over a preexisting structure.

The structure in question looked like a medieval cathedral. Some sort of Gothic, ancient building, the likes of which weren't anywhere in America. This was old—very old. Arched windows, detailed in quatrefoils and framed in stone, ran along one wall. Whatever was on the other side, it was too dark to see. The hallway stretched in both directions.

It was eerie and made more so by the silence that seemed to fill the hallway. It was lit by torches and candles in sconces in the walls, the only sound the quiet rushing of the fire burning.

Still, no answers to be had yet, so she grabbed Nick by the sleeve of his hoodie and tugged him to the right. Nick followed obediently in silence. They had gone about twenty feet before something caught their attention.

A statue in an alcove, tucked into the wall. Candles were

laid out at its feet in rows and tiers. That cinched it—this was definitely a church. Some strange, messed up, perverted church. Because what stood on the pedestal was not a statue of a saint or an angel, but of a *demon*.

At least, that was the only thing Lydia could come up with to describe it. It was a twisted, warped creature with wings of bone and claws that were far too long for its hands. Its face looked like a mask or a skull—or both. Its body looked like the carapace of an insect. Large, empty, gaping eyes and a fiendish, toothy maw that was threatening and gloating over a victory at the same time.

It had six arms. Four were held out at its sides at various angles, sharp claws in careful poses that seemed almost reminiscent of a statue of Shiva. It held a goblet in one clawed hand and was tipping it on its side, pouring its empty contents out into a waiting upturned talon. The flickering light of the candles added to its unnerving appearance.

"Toto, I don't think we're in Kansas anymore," Nick muttered.

Lydia had to agree and only nodded as they looked up at the monstrous statue.

An unexpected voice from behind them broke them of their awe and creeping dread.

"Hello, again."

SEVEN

"Hello, again."

Nick and Lydia screamed at the voice from behind them. In sync, they whirled, nearly toppling over each other.

It was that tall, pale vampire who had attacked them in Boston. Lyon—the Priest, as Aria had called him. "When I was told two of the marked had wandered out of the chamber, I had suspected it might be you." He wore a faint, sad smile on his porcelain features. "I apologize for upending you in such an undignified manner earlier."

They should run. Would it even do any good? She had no idea where she was. If Maverick and Aria were to be believed, they weren't even on Earth anymore. Nick seemed hell-bent on trying, at least. He took off running without a word, tearing down the hallway without looking at her. Either he'd assumed she'd follow, or he was too scared to care.

When she went to follow him, a hand clasped her upper arm. Lyon had firmly taken hold of her and kept her from making any progress. "Please, do not run. They greatly enjoy a hunt, and it will only exacerbate matters."

"They?"

"The Hounds."

That was like cold water running down her spine, and she felt her body go tense at the two simple words. *The Hounds.* "Oh God, Nick." She heard the sound of his heavy footfalls fade off into the distance as he ran away. "Please, don't hurt him!"

"He will be returned with a few scratches for his trouble. They will not damage him overmuch. But an escape attempt was foolish, I must admit." Lyon released his grasp on her arm, seeming to trust her not to repeat her friend's mistake. "Come." He headed off in the other direction. "I will make some tea."

Stay here and be hunted by the Hounds, go back to the cavern, or... drink some tea with a monster and maybe get some answers. That was why Lydia came out here, anyway, wasn't it? Answers?

Lyon stopped, turned halfway to look at her, and waited to see if she would follow him or run after her friend. Or maybe he expected her to collapse into a fit of hysterics. She kind of wanted to do all three.

Panic later.

Hiking up her proverbial breeches, she headed after Lyon. He watched her approach without moving. Suddenly, she realized why he was so eerie. Everybody shifted a little, even when they were holding perfectly still. Breathing, blinking or moving unconsciously. But Lyon just... didn't. More and more, he looked like a statue.

Lydia swallowed the rock in her throat. "Promise they aren't going to eat Nick. Promise you aren't going to eat *me.*"

Lyon's eyes creased in a gentle expression as he bowed his head before extended a hand to gesture down the hallway. "I give you my word neither will come to pass."

What the hell was happening to her life?

Here she was, wandering down a dark hallway of a marble church, or Gothic castle—or whatever—walking beside a tall, stoic, freak of nature. The more she watched Lyon, the more apparent it became he wasn't human. She couldn't help but stare, and then had to pull herself away from trying to figure him out to watch where she was going.

The white, tattooed writing that ran down the one side of his face started up in his hairline, ran down from his temple, down to his jaw. It then picked up again on his neck and ran down under the collar of his white shirt. His skin tone was only a bare shade darker than the white writing, making it almost impossible to see.

"Go on, then." Lyon broke the silence. "You are nearly boiling over with the need to speak."

"What are you?" She was glad she had brought her coat along with her, if only to shove her hands inside her pockets, wondering if she could climb the rest of herself in there to hide. "You're just like the thing that attacked me."

"Ah, yes. William. I apologize for his manners. He was overcome with hunger when he found you."

"Hunger?"

"We vary quite drastically in this world. William and I are creatures not still living, yet not quite dead. While all in this world may consume blood for pleasure, he and I are of a kind that requires it to maintain our strength. Especially young ones such as he."

"Are you *seriously* a vampire?"

"Hm?" Lyon looked at her curiously as if he wasn't quite sure what that word meant at first. Recognition dawned on him a second later. "Ah, yes, forgive me. I forget all the names in all the languages. No, I am not a vampire. Not as I believe you think of it." He paused. "Yet mayhap my kind are the wellspring from which those legends call their origin."

It took her a second to figure out what he meant. "Do you drink blood?"

"Yes."

"Do you have fangs?"

He paused reluctantly. "Yes."

"Then you're a vampire." She smirked. "If it looks like a duck and it quacks like a duck..."

Lyon looked as though he was amused, if begrudgingly so. "It is not nearly as simplistic as you may think." He shook his head. "I am detailing this to you out of order, I fear."

"I don't think there's a right order." Lydia looked off. The logical follow-up question begged to be asked. "How old are you?"

"Nearly two thousand years old."

Her steps hitched, and she almost stumbled over herself. She pulled up to a stop and couldn't help but stare at Lyon, wide-eyed.

He turned to look at her with a barely bemused expression. "I say that I am a monster who drinks blood, and you do not falter. I tell you my age, and that frightens you? You are an odd one."

"This is all bullshit. This all has to be bullshit. You're lying to me. Nobody is two thousand years old."

"I am not lying to you. Nor am I the eldest who lives in this world by far."

Lydia combed her hands through her hair. "I want to go home, please."

"Not even Master Edu could grant such a wish." There was pity in his voice as he watched her grapple with what he was saying.

"But why? Why are we here? Why have you hunted us down?" The fear building in her chest made her raise her voice.

Lyon lifted his hands, trying to insist that she calm down.

Taking a step back and leaning against the wall, feeling the cold marble at her back, she took a deep breath. This guy was telling her what she wanted to know. Screaming at him wasn't going to help. "Sorry."

"It is quite all right. This is no small matter, and you are not acting out of turn." He continued to lead her down the hallway. She followed him, having no real other option. "We do not mean you harm. We do not intend to hurt you in any way."

"Then what do you intend to do?"

Lyon paused speaking for a moment as if plotting out his words. The sorrow in his features had returned. "No souls are born in this place."

That took a second for her to process. It seemed like a jump in topics at first. She was sure it connected somehow. "You guys can't... make more of yourselves?"

"No. Nor do we die by normal means. We can be killed, but it is more difficult."

"That's why when I shot Edu, he just... came back?"

"Yes. You killed King Edu, but in such a way, it is a temporary state for us."

"Wait. I shot *the king*?" She snorted in laughter. It was the wrong time to laugh, but fuck it. That was funny.

Lyon chuckled and looked at her with a thin, barely-there smile. "Yes. You did. One who has not been felled in many centuries. He was quite impressed, if begrudgingly so. And, to be specific, you shot *a* king. This world has more than one, though they all slumber." He resumed walking.

She fell in step beside him as she considered what it must be like dying and coming back. "Does it hurt?"

"Of course."

Lydia winced. "That's awful."

"Yes, I suppose it can be."

"I suppose I should apologize if I see him again."

That brought another small chuckle out of him. "No, do not bother. He is a warrior, the most distinguished one to ever come from our world. He sees your act as something over which you should be proud, not ashamed."

Lydia smiled a bit. No, she didn't think she was ever going to be proud about shooting a man in the head. But at least she hadn't killed him—not for keeps, apparently. That was some peace of mind. "So, you take people to, what, refresh the gene pool? Bad choice of words, if you can't reproduce, I guess."

"Your sentiment is correct. Replenishment notwithstanding, to grow—to change—we must take." He gestured a hand in the air as he spoke. "If we are to progress and evolve, we must collect from your world when we are able."

"So, you take us, and then turn us into things like you?"

"Yes."

"How?"

"A ceremony. It is painless, I assure you."

"But what, exactly, happens?"

"I will wait to answer that until we are seated, if you do not mind."

Lydia knew he meant that to be comforting, but it didn't work. Not in the slightest. But since he was answering her questions, she could at the very least let the man—*vampire*—make her some damn tea. "Sure. I can wait. I guess."

"Thank you."

They crossed in front of another corridor, and it went on for a few feet before being consumed in darkness. No candles were burning down that way, and it left the hall an empty, eerie void of impenetrable darkness.

Turning, she realized the candles behind them were extinguishing a few moments after they passed them. The lights seemed to be following them, illuminating what was needed and leaving the rest of the massive building cast in complete shadow.

"Is this whole place always this spooky?" She wrinkled her nose.

"Yes."

Laughing at his deadpan answer, she shook her head. "So, where am I?"

"We are in the Cathedral of the Ancients, in the city of Yej near the Ronde d'el Lin, and overlooking the great Red River." Lyon cast a glance at her again, at her bewildered expression, and the look on his face was almost glinting with the barest amusement. "The name of the world in which you find yourself is Under."

All right. If she was on board this crazy train, she might as well play along. "Under. So, where is this place in relation to Earth?"

"Think of Under and Earth as two planets which orbit each other. Following this analogy—and it is a metaphor, nothing more—the orbit of your world and ours is an eccentric one. Our worlds do not pass by one another, so much as our worlds pass *through* the other."

Okay. She opted not to question the crazy, just roll with it. "What happens when our worlds pass *through* each other?"

"Those who know how to move between them may do so freely."

"I—" The next question never had a chance to come out of her mouth. Lydia paused in front of a long hallway, becoming distracted from their conversation. Something in the darkness didn't look quite the same. The blackness seemed textured, for lack of a better word.

There was a sound coming from the hallway, like sticks, scraping on stone.

The darkness *moved.* Lydia took one step back away from it, as something in the shadows shifted. It looked like a pile of branches, a giant tangled mess of thin twigs that wove in and out of each other. But they were moving. Toward her and around themselves, like a tumbleweed.

Each of the sticks was an arm. Or a leg. Or maybe they

served the same purpose. At the end of each rod was a single talon, opposed on the other side by a matching, smaller thumb of a claw. They were grasping and grabbing on to the other legs and arms. By pivoting its wrists and elbows, it could move the whole in one direction or another.

With a slow, creeping horror, Lydia realized the creature's arms began at a claw, ran to a wrist, to an elbow, back to a wrist, and another talon... *with nothing in between.* Hand, wrist, elbow, wrist, hand. It was a tangled mass of double-sided arms. No single body lived at its center.

A beige shape appeared within it, pushing out from the stick-like limbs. It was the upper portion of a skull that didn't look like it had ever belonged to a person or any animal she recognized. It only had one nostril that bisected its upper jaw, and it had no teeth. The holes for the eyes were large and vacant.

The hands were holding onto the faded and yellowed skull, passing it from claw to claw as it pushed itself toward the end of the hallway and into the light.

"H-holy—holy *fuck*." Lydia backed into the wall on the other side as the creature crawled out from the darkness. It was also huge, taking up the whole of the width of the hallway. It shrank and expanded as it moved, pulling itself along the corridor by grabbing the stone trim of the door. It walked on its claws like a sea urchin, alternating using them as feet before pulling them up into its mass of tangled sticks for another purpose.

"It means you no harm."

"You keep saying that." She wanted to glance at Lyon and call *bullshit*, but she couldn't take her eyes off the thing that was moving closer to her. The skull it held in the center of its body was now being held out further from its center and toward her as if it were trying to look at her.

Grabbing one of its stick-like arms and using it to extend its reach, it slowly stretched out a single claw toward her. When Lydia made a small, startled cry and jolted in fear, it shrank back at her unexpected movement.

It was acting timid and afraid like an animal, trying to inspect something unusual and new. Every time she moved, it would shy away, compressing its size, and then reach back out. She had a cat once when she was a kid, and it did the same thing the day it met a lizard for the first time.

"It is called a graspling," Lyon said. "They are not overly aggressive."

"I hope you realize that's not helping." She stared at the creature in front of her, who seemed hell-bent on... well, *poking* her.

It had so many hands. Each of its longer opposable talons was five or six inches long.

"They do not stalk their prey. Grasplings lie in the darkness and wait for the foolish to step within them."

He had a funny opinion of what aggressive meant. "They eat people."

"Everything here does."

"Ooh, still not helping..." Whimpering, she pulled back tighter against the wall. It was reaching out toward her again, a single claw grasping at the empty air. *Graspling*. Right. The name made sense. It almost looked like the hand of a chameleon, the way its digits moved.

It went to touch her face, and she let out a small cry and shifted to the side. Reaching up to protect her face, it gently grabbed hold of her hand. The claw was sharp, but it wasn't squeezing down to hurt her.

The creature seemed content with just squeezing and releasing her hand, then tried working its way up to her wrist. It was investigating her, trying to figure her out. A second talon stretched out and poked her in the shoulder.

It was standing close to her now, almost caging her against

the wall. It was a beaver dam of tangled arms, bending and twisting to create its shape. It had a musty, decrepit smell as if it had spent a great deal of time in a basement somewhere. The smell of dust made her want to sneeze as it crept nearer in its fascination.

"Please. That's close enough." She tried to sound firm but failed miserably. But damn it, she tried. "I'm having a rough day already." Hopefully, it could understand her. But that'd never stopped her before. She talked to everything. Animals, plants, dead bodies, her computer. So, she talked to the graspling now.

Remarkably, it inched backward. But while it stopped its advance, it didn't stop poking at her. It was now holding the edge of her coat. Thankfully, after a few more moments, the creature's curiosity seemed sated. Like an animal having enough of being petted, it just turned around and moved back into the darkness of the hallway from which it had emerged.

It left her finally aware her heart was pounding in her ears, her breath was short and fast, and she was trembling. She had always said "panic later" as her mantra, and now that the immediate threat was past, her body had decided that now was a perfect time for *later*.

The world threatened to drop her down a tunnel; she was going to pass out. *Breathe, you idiot!* Breathe in, breathe out.

A hand on her shoulder made her jump, and she whipped her head up to see Lyon standing next to her. He almost looked sympathetic, the slightest overlay of emotion on his alabaster features.

Pressing her palms into the cold stone of the wall behind her helped calm the swirling in her head. She kept breathing slowly, in and out. When she felt like she could move without hitting the floor, she nodded to him that she was now hopefully out of the woods.

He removed his hand and took a step back.

She was afraid to ask. But she had to know. "How many more creatures like that live in Under?"

Lyon let out a single laugh through his nose. He shook his head as if amused by a question only a child would ask. "Let me make you that tea." His non-answer was enough of a hint.

Whatever Under was, whatever its purpose might be... it was a world of monsters.

EIGHT

Edu had no patience.

That was an inarguable and intractable fact, one Edu never contested. It was not a trait he had any care to learn or practice, and now was no different.

He stood in the center of the great hall, looking up at the massive and tangled orrery overhead. It was a beautiful sculpture and would have been an awe-inspiring masterpiece alone, without the added use of its function. The purpose it served was vital to this world.

Shame he never had the resolve to understand it.

Yet he had others who filled that role. Since there were those who served him who could understand its movements, it was rendered moot that he could not comprehend the twisting tracks of brass and copper in their gyroscopic and nonsensical orbits about the center.

Perhaps if it had been a traditional orrery with predictable motions and movements on a single axis of rotation, he would have had the patience to learn. Edu was not a fool—he was not the idiot that many would paint him. He simply did not care to ply his time to such uses that others could far more readily fulfill.

Not a single track of the dozen or more shapes of glass and stone could be considered traditional. Each was oblong, warped, or twisted. And the movements were not steady. They could speed up or slow down, twist on an axis and whirl wildly about the center. Some days, the structure hardly resembled its appearance from the day prior. Other times, it could go for years with barely any adjustments at all. In truth, it did not even have a center around which the items pathed. It could tilt and swing one direction or the other, as the balance did the same.

The massive, hanging piece—easily twenty feet in diameter, suspended far overhead—displayed more than the simple rotation of planets. The orrery exhibited the shifts of power in Under and all the hidden workings in their world, not merely whether Under and Earth were in phase. The alignment of Earth and his world was a moment of diversion for him and carried no dread.

It was the movement of another piece upon the track that he eyed warily.

It was the track of one dark glass orb, impenetrable in its blackness and without any other tone or shade of color. All other representatives upon the structure were marbled—green, blue, purple, and white orbs were present, though they had not moved in centuries. His own familiar red swirled about the center, glistening in the amber light of the chamber.

The black orb had shifted unexpectedly. Now, it was quickly ticking steadily closer toward the center. Edu needed no assistance in divining what that meant. He had seen it happen frequently enough now that even *he* could discern its meaning.

Edu's hands clenched to fists at his sides, the leather straps of his armor creaking.

Aon would soon wake.

* * *

Lydia kind of hated tea.

But she didn't have the heart to tell the man who had brewed a cup the way it used to be done, by putting the leaves directly into the pot and straining it out into a glass for her.

So, she thanked him and lifted it to her lips. It had an earthy and tart smell to it. The taste wasn't too bad, she had to admit. Just a little bitter, offset with a herbal fullness. It wasn't too cloying or flowery, which was what she generally disliked in tea. Lyon had put out a small tray of odd-looking fruit, and she had picked a few of the things closest in resemblance to grapes and munched on them. They tasted unusual but fine.

Besides, the act of making her a pot of tea and trying to make her comfortable seemed to please the vampire, or whatever he was. Lyon had a contented look on his face for the first time—although the man had the range of emotions of a rock. They were so subtle, they were barely there.

He had taken her to a kitchen that looked like it saw decent use. He had apologized for the state of the room, and she had almost laughed at how polite he was being. The man had exceedingly practiced manners, something that betrayed that he probably was as old as he said he was.

He had left her to sit on a stool at a large, wood-topped counter in the center of the room while he brewed the tea. Sections of it were worn to different heights, so well-used was the thick wood surface.

"We do not usually take guests into the kitchen." It sounded like he was apologizing to her.

"I'm a prisoner, not a guest." Her response had sent Lyon into silence. She almost felt bad at hurting his feelings.

Watching him brew the tea let her sit for a few minutes and gather her thoughts. The kitchen looked like it belonged in a castle, like everything else here. An enormous hearth dominated one wall, the unevenly made bricks blackened from use. Wrought iron swing arms sat in heavy brackets, supporting a collection of massive pots and cauldrons with ease.

The room smelled of smoke and cooked food like a campfire. When Lyon had gone to boil the water, he had placed a pot over a more traditional stove and clicked it on, the ranging making a familiar click-click-click as the pilot light ignited the gas.

They had electricity. But also used candles and torches for light.

"This place is a hodge-podge," was her genius observation. A blender sat next to an old-fashioned wooden mortar and pestle. Each looked as used as the other. A gas range any chef would love to own, next to a massive, medieval hearth.

"Correct." He sat across from Lydia at the counter and fixed his cup of tea. "And serves true for more than just this kitchen. We collect from Earth that which interests us. But as we do not age and die as you do, we tend to keep a fondness for the antiquated." He gestured to the place around them. "Much as you observed this room is a collection of times and influences of others, so is our world as a whole. We progress and evolve in our own right, but we also collect from your world when we are able."

In some weird and twisted way, that was all starting to make sense. How all the prisoners seemed precious and exciting to them. Why they were very concerned about the injury on her arm becoming infected, or why that graspling creature had wanted to see what she was.

If nothing new ever happened here and nobody here ever aged or died, it must be like being trapped in purgatory.

Wait.

"Am I—is this—" She clasped the tea in her hands a little harder. "Is this Hell?"

Lyon laughed at that, a low but mirthful sound, and shook

his head. His laugh was pleasant and felt like a warm fire in a small room. When his laughter stilled, he had a genuine smile on his face. He may be a monster, but it was hard to be afraid of him. "No, my dear. This place far predates that name. While those you meet here have inspired many of the myths and legends your people tell of a dark place that lives below, fear not. You are not in the afterlife."

Lydia let out a breath and sipped her tea again. It was helping her feel better, honestly. It took some of the shaking out of her hands. And she hadn't eaten since, well, she didn't know. Dinner at the bar? How much time had passed since then?

"Every culture of yours has tales of demons, of monsters and outlandish creatures. When your world and Under touch, we may pass in between them. While the stories may not match the truth, the inspiration comes from us." He stirred his tea.

They sat in silence for a long moment as she processed everything he'd said. She wouldn't believe him if it weren't for the fact that she had seen proof to the contrary with her own eyes. All of it was real. And because of that, she had no reason to doubt him, even if it would be a lot easier to live in denial.

"And you're positive Nick is okay?" She chewed her lip.

"I promise you." He cast her another gentle, barely-there smile.

"What happens to us now? We're going to 'join' you, fine, but how, exactly?"

"We will take you to the Pool of the Ancients."

"The Ancients?"

"The original creatures who ruled this world, long before recorded time. They are the source of all that we are. Our primordial gods, for lack of a better word." He gestured idly.

"We go to the Pool of the Ancients. Then what happens?"

"The Ceremony of the Fall, where you will be shown what path you may take. Think of it as induction into our world. A homecoming. While its outcome may take many forms, it is not to be feared. You will emerge reborn and anew." The creases at the corners of his eyes deepened a little as he smiled. He meant it. This was a celebration to them.

The Fall. The man in Lydia's nightmare—Aon—had used that word. Fall. He had said she had not yet *Fallen.*

Lydia felt the color drain out of her face as she looked at Lyon, wide-eyed. Aon had claimed to be real. But she had written his existence off as her stress manifesting itself. But there was no way in hell she could have invented the Fall.

He was real.

The dream was real.

Shit.

"What is wrong?" Lyon's brow furrowed. "I assure you, it is a metaphorical fall from your world into Under. It is not meant literally. We do not throw you from a cliff."

Aon had warned her. If she told anyone about him, they'd kill her. But how did she know that was true? How could Lydia be sure the freak in her dreams didn't simply want to kill her personally instead? In a world of monsters, who was she supposed to trust?

Should she tell him about the man she had seen? Who had stalked her, then rammed his metal hand into her ribcage?

"Are you quite all right?" Lyon reached out a hand to place it on hers.

"Y-yeah." She looked down and sipped her tea again. "Sorry. It's just a lot to take in." It was a roll of the dice, taking a shadowy nightmare's word over trusting the morose tea-making vampire across the table from her, but she didn't exactly want to volunteer to put her head on a chopping block. She didn't know the rules of this place yet. She tried to change the subject back to the topic at hand. "So, you throw us into a Pool of Ancients—"

Lyon chuckled. "You walk in, I assure you. And it is the Pool of *the* Ancients."

"Sure. Whatever." It was all the same to her. "Do we all come out looking the same? I mean, mostly, you look human, give or take."

"Some, yes. Some... no."

The graspling. It had understood English and heard what Lydia had said. Fear yanked at her again. "That thing in the hallway."

"Yes."

Now that she was putting it all together, she wasn't happy about the picture the puzzle was beginning to form. She put her head in her hands and took a moment. They were going to pitch them into a pool, and they were going to come out as monsters. Human or inhuman. "I don't want to be a graspling. Please, let me go home."

"I cannot. You were chosen by the Ancients. The mark upon your arm—which appears upon all of those we now claim —shows you are destined for this. Not even Master Edu can go against their wishes." He pulled her hands away from her face and held them gently in his cold grasp.

"What... what'll I turn into?"

"I do not know. None of us know the path the Ancients have chosen for you."

Myths and monsters. Demons and ancient gods. The fact that everything here ate people—and if they didn't die when they were consumed? "Are you all food for those creatures? Is that what we're supposed to become?"

"That is a matter you will find upsetting." He was obviously trying to keep her from the brink of panic again. "It is complex. Wait and see what you will become before you judge how you may feel."

"How complex can it get, you damn pansy?" a male voice said from behind her. "They hunt, they eat, we die, we come back. We hunt them, we eat, they die, they come back. And so on. Done. Simple. Bam."

Lydia turned a little too quickly on the stool to face the source of the voice and nearly wound up on the ground. It teetered up onto two legs before she could grab the edge of the counter and steady herself.

The man who stood there had dark hair swept up and back, carefully gelled into place. He was wearing a red T-shirt under a black leather coat with loud, steel zippers. His shirt was shoved into jeans. The guy looked like he walked off a stage production of *Grease.*

"Hey, toots." He grinned at her. Yep. Definitely *Grease.* Smack in the middle of his left cheek was a red ink mark. It looked like the same writing as, well, everything else.

"Tim." Lyon let out a heavy sigh. "Leave her be."

"I ain't here for her, Priest." Tim walked up to the counter next to her and leaned on it heavily with both arms. He was unimpressed by Lyon, if not unimpressed by everything around him. He scooted closer to her and winked and pointedly went from looking at her, down her shirt, then back to her. "Or maybe I'll change my mind."

Lydia put her hand on his arm and pushed him the other direction. "Back off, douchebag."

Tim let out a sharp laugh and did as he was told, moving back without an argument. "Spunky. Maybe you'll end up in our house."

"House?" She still felt lost in the dark. Aon had mentioned the House of Words in her dream, but Lydia still had no idea what that meant.

Tim ignored her. "Anyway, Priest, Edu sent me here to tell you to get on with it already."

Lyon stood from the counter. "There are only a few gathered yet. When last he ruled over the Ceremonies, he was quick to denounce our methods over the number of them he was required to attend. I assumed he would wish to wait until we had hunted more."

"I don't ask questions." Tim shrugged and reached over the counter to grab a handful of the not-grapes and started popping them into his mouth, not hesitating to speak while chewing. "He said, 'Tell him to begin now,' and so, here I am, telling you to begin now."

Lyon grunted, clearly irritated but attempting to take it all in stride. He pulled on the bottom of his long white coat. "Very well. Then, Tim, since I now have much to do in short order, I ask you to return the young lady to the chamber with the others."

"Gladly." Tim grinned at her again.

Lyon's voice was quiet and stern as he spoke. "I will remind you, they are not to be touched until after the Fall. Desecrating the collected before they are cast is—"

"Punishable by true death," Tim finished for him. "I get it. I get it. Ruin my fun. C'mon, toots."

With that, Lydia was ushered out. There wasn't any point in running—or complaining—as she walked beside Tim down the hallway back the way she had come earlier with the Priest. "He said you couldn't die. So, what good is punishment by death?"

Tim slowed to walk next to her and was smirking. He was far more expressive than Lyon. Everything about Tim screamed that he was from the 1940s, so she didn't even need to ask Tim from when or where he hailed. He shoved his hands into the pockets of his leather coat. He reminded her way too much out of something from *West Side Story*. "I said *true* death. We can die for real. Nobody's ever born here, so if you can manage real murder, it's a huge crime."

Lydia was silent for a moment, watching him—wondering. Nobody was ever born here, and real death was complicated. One more thing was bugging her, though. One more thing she didn't understand. "What's with the facial tattoos and the masks?"

"Class system." Tim sniffed. Lyon was all flowery, philosophical language. Tim was not so complicated. "Everybody's got these marks." He pulled the collar of his shirt away from his neck so that she could see the symbols and etchings that were written on his skin in red ink.

"I'll need more than that. What's a mark *for?*" She rolled her eyes. He was blunt. But he was also being purposefully dense.

"Marks are power. The more marks, the more powerful the person. This," he pointed at his face, "is called a soulmark. Everyone has at least one. Doesn't matter. If you're super special, you get to cover it with a mask."

"The more soulmarks you have..." She hovered over the words, not honestly believing what she was saying. It sounded so stupid in her head, and saying it aloud made it worse. "The bigger the mask to cover them?"

"Not bad, toots!" He laughed. "And they say the cute ones are dumb."

"Shut up."

"Eh. Nah, don't think I will. So, you know if you see somebody with a mask, they're somebody important. Those of us without them, they call us servants." He shrugged. "I think it's stupid, but nobody asks me."

"Why cover the soulmarks, though?" She appreciated how casual Tim was, if nothing else.

"A couple of reasons. First, it's how you really kill us. Take these off, then we're as good as human again. Second..." Tim trailed off, trying to figure out how to explain it. "Second, it's like seeing someone's soul. Which's why they call it that. If you could read it, you could read everything you'd ever need to know about the person. It's worse than being naked."

"What're the different colors for?"

"Different houses. There are six houses. Blue, black, purple, white, green, and red, like mine. Just designates where your power comes from and how it manifests. We all tend toward different things." The way he said it made it clear this was all basic shit to them.

Sure, why not? White belonged to priests who were actually vampires, and as far as she could tell, red made you kind of a dick. Lydia decided not to voice that last part. "Can you read them?"

"Nah. Nobody can. But besides as a kind of armor, the masks are a tradition. There are a lot of stupid traditions here. You'll get used to it. But people'd rather be naked around here than take off their masks. Trust me. People *love* to be naked around here." His grin turned lascivious with the clear innuendo.

"First, no. Second, what the hell is that supposed to mean?" She walked a step farther away from him.

"It means nobody here can ever get sick or die. That nobody here can get pregnant. That people here don't age, are basically immortal, and get *really* bored. Maybe it's 'cuz I'm in the House of Flames, but we spend a lot of time amusing each other, if you get my drift."

"So, you're a bunch of perverts."

"Yeah." His grin didn't waver. "Yeah, we are."

"That wasn't a compliment." She really wanted to smack the expression off his face.

"I know."

Lydia put her hand over her eyes and sighed. This man was impossible. But she was having a healthy, human conversation with him, and something about it was disarming. It made her not so terrified of the shadows that clung to them as they walked.

The candles were still doing that creepy only-lit-when-they-were-near thing, and the hallway, although less foreign than the first time she saw it, was no less unnerving. "Red is the House of Flames? What're the other colors called?"

"Aren't you just brim full of questions?"

"I'm a prisoner in a world of monsters, so sue me if I have questions."

"Right, fine, but what'll you give me in return?" There was that innuendo again. "Pay up, or I shut up, toots."

"Literally nothing." She shot him a glare.

He let out another loud laugh and shrugged and called her bluff. It seemed like the explanations were going to stop there unless she paid up, and she wasn't, under any circumstances, going to do anything of the sort.

Polished marble hallways turned to rough-hewn stone. Before long, Tim was pushing open the large wooden door to the chamber they were all kept within. "See ya later, babe." He winked as she walked past him.

"Yeah, bye, dickwad."

All conversation had ceased as the door had opened, and all eyes were turned on her. She felt like she was just thrust out onto a stage without knowing any of her lines. Clearing her throat, she ducked her head and headed toward the wall where Nick, Gary, and Kaori had been before she had struck off on an adventure.

"Oh, goodness!" Gary greeted her as he shot to his feet and stepped toward her. His hands fell on her shoulders. "We were so worried."

"I wasn't." Nick was sitting on the floor, clearly pissed.

"Oh God, Nick, are you okay?" She pushed away from Gary to see her friend.

Nick was sitting against a rock. One of his pant legs was rolled up with a cloth tied around his calf. "I'm fine. Cut up. But fine. There were demon-dogs. They fucking chased me, Lyd."

"I'm sorry?" Why did she feel guilty? Why the hell was Nick glaring at her like this was her fault? She hadn't done anything wrong.

"I'm not going out there again." He folded his arms across

his chest. Oh. Lydia got it now. He was pissy because he'd been roughed up. Nick got like this when he felt like he was being dealt a lousy hand.

"So, what happened to you?" Gary asked, prying desperately for any news. And, oh boy, did she have a story to tell him.

Too bad everything she'd learned turned out to be too little, too late.

"Well—" She was interrupted by the sound of ringing in the background. It sounded like large church bells, muffled and far away. It was more of a vibration in the stone walls than anything else. She was the only one in the room who knew what it meant.

For as little as she understood about what this place meant or about who these people were?

The Ceremony of the Fall was starting.

NINE

Everything was a flurry of motion.

As it turned out, groups of people didn't like to be abducted, herded into a room, left in the dark about what was happening, and then rounded up like cattle.

They kinda took offense to that and didn't react too politely about the whole scenario.

Figures in white filed into the room, led by a painfully thin old woman in a birdlike white half mask. Behind them came a small horde of—

Oh.

Those would be the Hounds, then. Lydia had yet to see any of them herself, but judging by Gary's and Nick's reactions, that was what they were.

The monsters walked on all fours, backs hunched and covered in damp, scraggly fur. They had odd, bone-like faces with teeth that were far too long for their jaws. On one side of their faces, they had four eyes, and on the other, only two. They were snapping their massive jaws in excitement. It made a horrible clicking noise as they chattered.

The monsters of Under had come prepared for a reluctant

bunch of prisoners. The Hounds were moving around the edges of the rooms, climbing over the rocks and up onto the walls, clinging to the stone surfaces as though they had every business in the world defying gravity.

They almost looked like vultures with their bald heads and what looked like fur, or feathers, bushing out from their shoulders and down their hunched bodies. After a moment, it became clear what they were trying to do. The Hounds were circling the room, then moving inward—herding them all into the center.

Kaori was weeping quietly, still huddling against Nick like she had known him all her life. Nick was holding her, trying to console the poor woman as they were pushed away from the walls by the monsters pushing them toward each other to avoid the beasts.

Gary was holding onto Lydia's arm like a kid in a haunted house.

"Where are they taking us?" Nick's voice was tight with fear. Any annoyance he had in Lydia's direction was gone the moment a real threat appeared.

The monsters were starting to push them closer to the door, getting them together and ensuring there were no strays. They were dogs herding sheep.

"This world collects people—" It was hard to sum everything up quickly. "They turn us into monsters like them. They're going to add us to their ranks." It felt weird, trying to explain things when she didn't have an excellent understanding of it either. Just what she'd briefly been told by Lyon and Tim, for what good it did. Certainly didn't save any of them from what was going to happen.

"It is time!" The woman in the bird mask gestured broadly with her thin, frail hands. The robes hung loosely off her skeletal frame. Seeing her up close, the woman's face was cracked and wrinkled. "We will now welcome you all to our world. We will welcome you all *home*."

All her words did was set off a panic in the crowd. The frightened mass of people pressed back toward the Hounds, who snapped and slashed at them, driving them back into each other in a muddled and tangled mess.

The woman in the mask whirled and walked from the room, long, flowing robes trailing behind her. That was their cue to move, and nobody wanted to do so of their own accord. Someone behind her screamed as one of the dogs jumped forward, driving them closer to the door.

A few of the brave in the group decided to plod after the woman in white, processing past others in white clothing who were standing to either side. Lydia, personally, was just sick of getting shoved and being so shoulder-to-shoulder with everyone. It wasn't bravery, it was a growing sense of claustrophobia that drove her forward.

Gary was still clinging to her arm and walked beside and behind her a step. "They're going to make us like them? Immortal, powerful creatures?"

"Well... yeah, I guess?" Lydia blinked at Gary's optimistic view of the situation. She opted not to tell him about the "or maybe a total freak of nature" part of it.

"How exciting!" Gary's declaration was an enthusiastic whisper. When she looked at him agog, he stammered, "I mean, that's not—I don't mean that I feel we... I mean—"

"Oh, stop." She found herself smiling. "You love this."

"It's—I live a very dull life with my two cats and a flatmate I rarely see. I fear very little interesting happened to me, until now." He looked sheepish for a moment. "Never did I think anything like this would ever happen to me. Even if they mean to kill us, this is all terribly, well, thrilling. I do hope my cats will be all right."

"I'm sure they'll be fine." She liked this guy and would love to have sat down and listened to him rant on some topic or another over coffee. But that wouldn't likely ever happen now. "I would have liked to have been your friend, Gary."

"And I you, Lydia. Perhaps we still will." He still sounded excited, even as he was clutching to her arm like a monster was going to come leaping out of a shadow to terrorize them at any moment.

Well, maybe one would.

She opted not to tell Gary about the graspling.

Minutes passed with them being herded down the hallway. Lydia hadn't come down this way with Lyon; she had no idea where they were. Glancing back over her shoulder, Nick was still walking with Kaori huddled against his chest, her head lowered and a hand over her eyes. Poor thing must be exhausted, spending this entire time on the razor's edge of panic.

Nick caught her gaze, and he, too, looked worn thin. He shrugged and kept an arm around the girl. It felt like they were being led to the slaughter. Even with what she knew—that they'd come out the other side as changed versions of them-selves—it still felt like death.

They were going to Fall.

A few minutes later, they arrived at—yeah, that was a pool, all right. It was more like an underground lake. The pack of confused prisoners were forced to spread along the shore as the Hounds kept nipping at their heels, pushing everyone out of the corridor to stand at the edge of the liquid.

She wouldn't go so far as to call it water. It was glowing red.

Lydia had watched a documentary special on species of phosphorescent creatures, and this looked very much like that. The glow came from within the water itself, as though there was some kind of bacteria in the liquid that was letting off a faint red light.

While the liquid at the edge of the lake was calm, there were faint waves that began to grow the farther it stretched ahead of them. Ripples from a massive, hundred-foot waterfall that sat at the far end of the lake, the source of which were three *massive* heads. Skulls or exoskeletons, Lydia couldn't tell. Like everything else she had met or seen, their features were ghastly and overblown—strange and exaggerated.

From their jaws or eye sockets poured the glowing red liquid, casting their vicious features in a dim and unfocused light that left the whole thing looking like something out of a horror show.

Then she realized the walls of this cave were different than the rest of the hallways she had seen. Everything had a weird kind of bumpiness to it she didn't understand at first. Then, slowly, it dawned on her what she was looking at. The walls of this cave, even the ceiling and the shoreline, were comprised of masks and skulls. Here, it was hard to tell the difference between them.

It was a catacomb. A lake in a giant cavern, constructed entirely from the dead. Each one different from the last, each one the remains of a strange and foreign creature. She wasn't the only one who noticed. A cry of terror broke out through the crowd, and several tried to turn and flee.

But the Hounds were there to stop them. They were faced with the decision between the intangible fear of what the lake represented and the very tangible fear of the monster dogs.

There was a murmur from the darkness, and Lydia turned to look along the shore, realizing they weren't alone. There were crowds of people hovering in the shadows just out of view of the glow from the lake. Their group of prisoners were outnumbered by the creatures looming in the darkness—people and monsters alike. It was hard to pick anything out of the crowd, just a mass of people standing and watching. Some wore masks; many did not.

Jutting out into the lake was a large, circular platform, like the ruins of a Greek temple. It was polished stone and one of the few surfaces that looked not to be made out of the remains of the dead.

It was at the edge of the stairs leading to this platform that they were all now clumped. Up the small flight of polished steps, white dress gleaming red in the glow of the lake around them, stood the old woman.

Behind her, arranged about the circle of the platform, were seven pedestals that were on a separate small jut out from the circular platform. Each dais had a statue upon it. In front of each of the sculptures, save one, was a figure.

She recognized Edu quickly. It was hard not to, as he was standing there in full armor, dwarfing the others in his sheer scale. He stood with his sword in front of him, tip resting on the ground, his gauntleted, clawed hands folded over the pommel of the blade. He looked like some demonic knight from the cover of a bad heavy metal comic book. The statue that loomed behind him was of some great dragon, which resembled the armor he wore.

And there was Maverick. He was not wearing the medical equipment she had seen him in earlier. Instead, he wore a turn-of-the-century suit in brown and purple. He was standing in front of another one of the massive statues. His hands were clasped in front of him, and his expression was analytical and curious as he looked out at the crowd of huddled prisoners. The remaining four were strangers.

One short, pudgy man in all white and gold wore a birdlike mask resembling that of the old woman. It went across the middle of his face like a strap, only serving to give him a beakish nose and doing absolutely nothing to help the fact that he suddenly reminded her of the Penguin from *Batman*. And just as sleazy-looking, to boot.

The next was a woman with long white hair, pulled back and clipped in careful curls and waves. She wore an antiquated blue dress. Her pure white hair caught the reflection of the lighting around her and was a sharp mismatch to her young, beautiful face. Her Venetian mask obscured only her forehead and down the bridge of her nose, leaving—uncommonly, so far —both her eyes exposed. Her expression was placid and empty.

The next person she didn't recognize was a woman with long, braided, and beaded dark hair. She was barely clothed, wearing only a loincloth that stretched down to the floor. She was actually pretty much topless, revealing plenty of her tanned skin, with only scraps of jewelry and fabric hanging off her upper body in portions that left nothing to the imagination. She was leaning back against her statue with her arms crossed over her ample chest, looking utterly bored. Her green wooden mask covered the upper half of her face and protruded back into her hair to form two small sets of horns Lydia hoped were only decorative.

A broad-shouldered man in all black stood next to her. His bald head had scars that traced along over the edge of his ear and down his face. His mask covered more than just the side of his face but went up along half his skull and around to the back. His clothing was an expensively tailored black suit, playing perfectly against his dark-toned skin, with details added by changing the sheen of the texture of the garment. He reminded her keenly of Aon.

The statues the figures stood in front of were no friendlier than the six people themselves. She wondered why somebody was missing. There were seven statues, but six people.

An overhead source of light that might be moonlight casting through a rock landed perfectly onto the circle of figures. They were illuminated in the stark difference of crimson from below and turquoise from above, leaving the rest in a ruddy, faint purple.

"We greet you, Children of the Ancients!" The old woman gestured dramatically again like she was in the middle of some ancient Greek stage, performing an epic tale. "Welcome to the Ceremony of the Fall."

Lydia noticed Lyon standing at the far end of the platform. He was nearly out of the light. The seven platforms and statues were arranged such that it left a path up and through the center, and then down onto the other side. Another set of stairs were on that far side, leading into the lake of glowing crimson liquid. He was standing up to his ankles in the ooze, watching the group of them with a passive expression.

Someone in the group decided to make a break for it. They pushed their way out of the pack and turned toward the tunnel through which they had come. A Hound leaped to block his path, and when he tried to dodge, the dog tackled the man to the ground and pinned him roughly to the floor with a massive claw. The beast pushed the man's face into the dirt and snapped its jaws toward his neck. It was clear the Hound wished to tear him to pieces.

But they were needed, every single one of the prisoners. And even the dog seemed to know that, and it snarled in annoyance before climbing off the man. The man in question scampered across the floor, trying desperately to return to the false safety of numbers. The dog snapped its jaws, chittering them together in hunger and annoyance.

"Escape attempts are all in vain, but your future is bright. Turn away from your fruitless, empty world of rot and disease, where all must wither away. Do not despair, Children, for you now come to your true path. Here in this world, you will find meaning the likes of which you could only aspire, and power beyond your wildest dreams." The bird woman gestured again while she dramatically orated. "Who will seek their new life first?"

Nobody answered. Well, not for the first beat, anyway.

"I-I—" Gary stepped forward. "I will."

"Gary?" Lydia blinked, stunned.

"I've only ever *read* stories. I've never been a part of one." Gary smiled at her meekly. He turned back to the bird woman.

"Come forward, brave child." She held out her hand to him.

Gary did as she said, steps timid and unsure. He looked like he was going to leap out of his skin at any moment, but he was the only one ballsy enough to step forward.

The bird woman was still smiling as she stepped aside and gestured for Gary to walk across the platform. He did, even if he spent the entire time glancing at the six dramatically lit—and dramatically dressed—figures arranged around the circle.

Gary headed across the platform to where Lyon stood, and Lydia could hear him quietly greet the taller man. He struck out his hand as if to shake Lyon's. Even in a moment where he might be facing death, he was still unflinchingly British.

Lydia found her hands had made their way over her mouth, and she desperately wished for Gary not to die. Desperately hoped he would somehow be saved. Or whatever was about to happen, let it not be so bad.

Lyon looked down at the man's hand, and Gary, realizing his silliness, laughed nervously and pointed into the water. Lyon merely nodded once.

Gary stepped forward, and she watched as he picked his way down a flight of stairs she could not see, descending into the glowing liquid. When it moved, it looked viscous. The waves coming off him were thick and slow.

When he had made his way down to his waist, he paused.

Something grabbed him and tore him under the liquid. His startled cry was cut off as he was abruptly dragged beneath the surface.

The crowd screamed.

So much for that.

TEN

Gary was gone. Disappeared beneath the waves.

The crowd shrieked and pressed backward against the Hounds, who snapped and made hissing, rasping, barking sounds at them in response, keeping them trapped.

The room hung in silence. The seconds dragging on.

Lydia counted to ten. *Oh, please, Gary... don't be dead.*

Finally, a figure began to emerge from the crimson liquid. A shape moved under the water briefly before breaching the surface. An audible gasp for air rang out in the room.

Gary pulled himself up the stairs, coughing and wheezing. Lyon was there to assist him, grasping him under the arm and pulling him to his feet.

When the Englishman stood, the left quarter of his face, from over his nose down to his jaw, was covered with a deep purple mask. It was featureless and unadorned, and she had no idea how it would have been stuck there if magic wasn't suddenly a real thing.

It was undoubtedly still Gary. Even with the mask, she recognized his face. His skin was paler, his hair was ruffled and wet, but it was him. He wobbled his way up the steps, and he looked unsteady and a little dizzy, but... fine. Queasy, but not dead.

Gary turned toward where Maverick stood, and he smiled that same slightly toothy, overzealous smile she had seen him wear a few times in her short time knowing him, and bowed to the doctor.

Maverick nodded once to the man in turn. As if this was any other day of the week.

Gary walked back down the steps, toward the crowd. As he approached the pack of prisoners, everyone parted for him—all except her and Nick. Kaori didn't really count, as she was now hiding behind Nick as desperately as she could.

"Gary?" She realized his eyes were now yellow, like Maverick's. "Is that... you?"

"Yes!" He laughed in delight. "Still me, I must say. Although I feel quite changed." Humming in thought, he looked off into the darkness. "Everything makes much more sense now. All those answers you went looking for, and now I have them. How charming. I—ah." Something caught his attention off in the shadows. "I must go. I do hope we'll chat later. Good luck, my friends!"

And with that, the Englishman strolled off, passing through the crowd of people who all moved aside, not wanting to go near the man who had gone in and out of the lake. He headed toward the gaggle of observers who were assembled near the shadows and began excitedly talking to someone who had stepped out of the darkness to meet him.

Aria. The woman had beckoned the recently-former-mortal over and was now holding his elbow, talking to him and gently gesturing for him to lower his tone.

"Are any others willing to step forward?" The bird woman interrupted Lydia's thoughts, dragging her back to the moment. "To accept the transformation peacefully is to take into yourself the exaltation of the Ancients. To fight is to bring yourself unnecessary fear."

Someone else stepped forward, a woman this time. Lydia didn't recognize her, and she could do little else but watch as the pattern repeated. The woman stepped into the water, disappeared under the liquid, and then re-emerged. This time, she wore no mask, and the markings on her face were in thin black lines.

The third person to step forward didn't have exactly the same experience as everyone else.

Any hope of the crowd going peacefully one by one into the glowing waters was dashed the moment the man who came out of the water... was no longer a man.

The creature that emerged looked like the crossbreed between an iguana and a praying mantis. A long, thrashing tail snapped back and forth behind a body held up on spindly legs. It weaved back and forth as it climbed up the stairs. Red liquid was dripping from its frame. Long, spindly arms cleaned its face, wiping the moisture from its faceted eyes set into the skull of a reptile. The thing was enormous, raising itself up to its full height at twelve feet or more, and roared at the crowd.

The sound was both a low rumble and a high, ear-piercing screech that left the group of prisoners ducking and covering their ears. No one else, none of those who belonged to this world already, reacted to the noise. It echoed and lingered in the large empty chamber for several seconds before fading off.

That sent the small group of prisoners into a panic. They screamed and fell back toward the Hounds, who had their work cut out for them, trying to keep the sudden mass of people in place.

"*Enough!*" The bird woman's shrill voice echoed in the hall. The monster—the man who had just become a monster, rather —had walked up behind her. She seemed unafraid of it as it loomed over her. "Do not fear but rejoice! For he, too, has found his path."

The lizard-bug-monster-thing stepped around the bird woman and off the platform in one easy step, long legs ticking against the polished stone surface and onto the dirt. It seemed uninterested in the rest of them. The prisoners scrambled to get out of its way as it headed for the exit. The Hounds did nothing to stop it, standing aside for the creature as it went down the darkness of the way they had come. It had a new life to pursue.

Shockingly, nobody volunteered after that.

Two men approached from the wings. They went to the first person they came across, grabbing them roughly by the arms and dragging them kicking and screaming up the stairs. Even though the man they had seized was a full-grown adult, nothing that guy could do—kicking, shouting, yanking backward to try to pull them off balance—seemed to do anything to affect the two others forcing him forward.

They weren't human, after all.

One by one, the prisoners were fed into the pond. One by one, people were grabbed from the pack and fed into the pool. One by one, they emerged as monsters—or as beasts pretending to be people. It didn't matter.

Then, they came toward where Nick, Kaori, and Lydia had huddled in the crowd. The approach of the two men sent Kaori wailing into hysterics, and she ducked behind Nick once more, cowering behind her friend.

The men went to grab Nick.

"Wait—" Lydia stopped them. The two men looked at her, obviously surprised. It might be pointless—it was only going to save Nick and Kaori a few minutes of time as humans—but damn it all, it felt noble. "I... I'll go."

The two men in white stood aside and let Lydia make good on her pledge. Swallowing through her dry mouth, she glanced back at Nick, who was wild-eyed in fear. He mouthed something, trying to speak, but couldn't find the words.

The man next to her cleared his throat and reminded her they were trying to keep to a schedule. Lydia took a deep breath, held it, and walked toward the steps. It was her turn now. She could do this. Over a dozen people already had. Maybe she'd come out as a big weird bug monster. Maybe she'd have superpowers.

Maybe a lot of things.

The polished stone steps in front of her felt immensely daunting as she stepped up to the top of the platform.

The bird woman was watching her, expressionless behind the gaping black holes she had for eyes. "Do not be afraid, my child."

Lydia didn't have the heart—or the ability—to explain to the woman exactly how little those words actually helped.

The platform around her felt massive and overwhelming. The six figures were watching her in various states. Some bored, like the nearly naked woman. Some curious, like the woman in the blue dress. Her arms were exposed, revealing long trails of the cryptic writing etched onto her skin in blue ink. Her eyes were pure white, lid to lid. She had worn an empty expression until this moment and seemed suddenly interested in Lydia's presence.

Her mask had scrollwork upon it like that of a classic Venetian masquerade piece. Curling leaves and acanthus scrolls accented in silver tones wound into her hair and blended together. It almost looked like a crown, the way her mask wove into her stark white hair and back through the carefully arranged curls.

In a twist to deep blue lips, the woman smiled at her. But as soon as the expression was there, it was gone, fading back to an emptiness that made the woman look like a statue, somehow even more so than Lyon.

But her moment to stop and think was gone, and the nudge at her back from one of the men in white prompted her to keep walking. Heading to the edge of the pool of glowing red liquid, she couldn't help but look at Lyon, hoping for some kind of shelter. Some sort of reprieve.

Lyon merely held his hand out to her—a gentleman, helping a woman down a flight of stairs.

Lydia was shaking again, and she felt short of breath. Oh God. This was worse than if they had pushed them off a cliff into the pool of glowing, luminescent crimson liquid. Maybe she should have fought and struggled. Being dragged in like the others would have been easier.

"I don't wanna be a freaky bug monster."

Lyon chuckled quietly.

Squeezing her eyes shut for a brief second, she felt the tears that she had been holding back escape. They ran down her cheeks, uninterrupted. She didn't bother to wipe them away. What was the point?

Lydia placed her hand in Lyon's. She was glad to feel him close his grasp around her and squeeze her hand. Trying, once more, to console her. This time, it wasn't effective.

She put her foot into the water. It seeped into her shoe, around her ankle, and into her socks. It wasn't cold or warm; it wasn't anything. Just wet. She stepped her other foot in and felt it start to soak up the edge of her pants. Next, step down, and it was up to her calves. Lyon released her hand so she could move past him.

"I will see you on the other side." Lyon's tone was compassionate and gentle. It must be hard, to treat people with kindness after living as long as he had. To spend two thousand years like this and still be able to be charitable. The stray thought drifted through her mind, briefly interrupting the fear.

Another step, and the water was up past her knees now. "Thanks, Lyon. Thanks for caring."

Another step and she was up to her waist. And, just like the others, something grabbed her. It wasn't so much of a hand, or a claw, as it was the liquid itself. Like a current of water, suddenly pulling her out and down, dragging her under the red liquid without any chance to let her wonder.

The crimson liquid filled her mouth before she could even try to close it to hold her breath or scream. It pushed into her like trying to drink from a hose, forcing itself down her throat and filling her stomach. It forced the air from her in one moment, as it seeped into every part of her.

Without warning and in one terrible moment, it filled her lungs, and nothing even left her as bubbles of air as it consumed her.

There was nothing to see but that eerie, red glow all around her. Thrashing, her heart pounding in her ears violently, she tried to struggle and push against the liquid all around her. It was thick, viscous, and the harder she moved, the harder it became to do so.

It didn't take long, though, for her body to begin to go numb. For her mind to quietly give in to the fact that she was drowning. That she was going to die. The liquid had pervaded every part of her, and the heartbeat in her ears was slowly fading.

It was peaceful, in a weird way. Just a pure encroaching nothingness. It was easy. It was binary. One moment, alive... the next, not.

At that moment, her mind conjured up one final memory.

Her mind conjured up that thought in a fruitless and desperate attempt to cling to whatever shard of life remained as it was being taken away. And since she was drowning, she had so very much time to ponder the gravity and meaning of that singular *thing* as she was now sinking deeper beneath the waves. No bother reaching. No bother breathing.

Only a memory.

It was a time she went fishing with her father's friend and his kids, standing on the beach, casting lures off into the pond. She must have been twelve, standing on the shore of a lake up in Vermont, trying to catch pickerel or trout. Her? All she could find were sunfish if she was lucky.

She'd been absolute crap at fishing. Couldn't cast right, couldn't reel in right, but they had put up with her patiently. It wasn't a particularly happy or unhappy memory. She hadn't thought about that day in Vermont since it had happened. Why, of all the last moments, would it have been that?

Maybe it was standing on the shore of this red lake that brought back that memory of fishing, standing on dirt shores in a sunny, Vermont forest. Maybe it was the vaguely violent act of fishing. Maybe it was the lake itself.

Her consciousness was starting to fade, hanging on that memory of the sun on the shore on that muggy summer day, with the buzz of mosquitos in the air.

Hadn't this gone on too long?

Wasn't she meant to come back up by now?

A fish had no business being on the shore.

She had no business being underwater.

That was the last thought she had as her world faded to darkness.

* * *

Aon flicked his fingernail against the glass tube of his machine. The troublesome air bubble that was clinging to the side of the cylinder obediently rose to the surface of the viscous liquid within.

It was not that it truly mattered. The blood was being filtered, and the results of his machine would be unaffected by such things. But, it gave him great pleasure to watch his mastery at work. It gave him great joy to hear it whir as it purified the ink from the liquid within it.

Almost as much joy as it brought him to procure the substance within.

Sobbing broke into a muffled scream behind him. His "patient" was once more demanding his attention. Turning on his heel, he regarded the man strapped to his metal table. The bronze-skinned warrior had been in his laboratory for several days now. He was on the verge of breaking—the verge of begging Aon for mercy. For release. He could have had such a confession by now if he wished, but these things should be savored, after all.

And besides, he did not need the man's submission.

He needed his blood.

The rest was merely for his own entertainment.

His own revenge.

"Really, the more you scream, the more you will simply tear the stitches loose." Aon tutted. Pulling his other black glove off, he tossed it onto the tray next to the table. Lifting a black thread and the thick needle meant for canvas sails, he looked down at the weak, nearly broken man beneath him.

The man only watched, wild-eyed and panicked, his body shuddering in pain and terror both. Blood was leaking from around his mouth, around the string Aon had used to stitch the man's mouth shut. The holes through which the thread wove were elongated now, tearing through the man's flesh as he screamed in agony.

Aon smiled beneath his mask.

How beautiful.

"See? You've torn them. Now I must replace them." Lifting a pair of scissors, he snipped the thread, uncaring for the flesh beneath. The man beneath him was no longer healing as fast as he should, but it would still only be a matter of hours before any cuts he gave the warrior would be gone. "Do be more careful with my handiwork, yes? I would hate to think you do not appreciate the care to which I am taking with you."

The man beneath him sobbed. Squeezed his eyes shut tight,

tears streamed from the corners and into his thick, sweat-matted black hair. Yes. He was close to the edge. Close to shattering. It wouldn't take long before the man's sanity was far more gone than even Aon's own.

But there was still much to enjoy before then.

Yanking the old thread loose from the man's flesh, Aon watched as the formerly grandiose warrior cried and whimpered in pain like a small child. Oh, how it lifted his heart to hear it. He leaned in, and with both hands, wiped some of the man's blood away from his lips with his bare fingertips. It would have been a gesture of compassion, if it were not Aon delivering it.

The warrior simply wept once more.

Turning his needle about in his left hand, he began the work of stitching the man's mouth back shut. New wounds, just to the left of the ones that were struggling to close. He began to hum to himself as he worked. A small, pleasant tune, one jarringly different in tone from the man's renewed wails of pain.

"Oh shush, Qta, or you will drown yourself in your own blood again."

Aon became aware of himself. Slipping from his memories and back into this dream state. This strange, barely-there awareness of himself in his own crypt where he slumbered. He was lying on his back where he should be, in his normal state of repose. But something was deeply amiss.

He was not alone.

It took him longer to realize that he had unexpected company than it should have. Normally, he would have become instantly aware of a presence beside him. But perhaps it was because the presence felt like a warm blanket over him, that he did not wish to rouse enough to understand what was happening.

A small frame—lithe and soft—rested there with him.

Their head was tucked up underneath his chin. A hand tangled in the fabric of his vest, clinging weakly. They were shivering as if they had crawled in close to him for warmth.

For protection. *For safety.*

No one came to him for any of those things.

No one ever came to him at all.

No one dared.

Lifting his head, he caught sight of long blonde hair that fell in waves along the black fabric of his clothing. His little dream thief had returned, it seemed. And this time, she had the audacity to crawl in beside him, to curl up resting atop him as though they were lovers.

A dangerous presumption.

For the single tick of a clock, he let himself enjoy it. Pushed away the alarm that was growing as he became more conscious. He held it at bay for only a moment.

The joy shattered as he came to one very inevitable conclusion.

Something was very wrong.

Carefully, he sat up, shifting her so she was lying down on her back. Her eyes were open, but they were glassy and unfocused. Seeing neither him nor this dream world, nor was awake.

She was nowhere at all. Her body was convulsing in fits as she shivered, her breathing short and shallow.

Her heartbeat—what he could sense of it—was thin and far away.

But the most troubling thing of all, was that he could no longer sense the mark she carried that made her one of the chosen humans to join their world of monsters and demons.

But she bore no ink on her face either.

She was human. *Mortal.*

And unmarked.

How could that be? She had clearly been chosen by the Ancients, but now was struck clean of their tarnish. Whatever manner of black magic that could have removed the mark from her flesh, he could not fathom. And such things were his area of expertise.

"You insist on continuing to become more interesting, don't you, my darling?" He had murmured his words, not expecting her to wake from her fever state. Her dreaming mind was struggling to hold on to life, let alone be aware of his words.

But his voice seemed to draw her out of her reverie, and she blinked. She tried to desperately focus on him, but she was gravely ill.

She was dying.

The thought hurt him.

His heart cinched in his chest, and he was taken aback for a moment at how suddenly he wished her to live. His little dream-thief. His little mystery. The chosen and now *abandoned* mortal. It had never happened, not once in his five thousand years of life. And to see her die before the conundrum could be solved? A tragic waste.

"Wh..." She could not form words.

He shushed her, leaning his head down close to hers. "You are unwell. You are dreaming again. Do not be afraid. This time, I mean you no harm."

Lydia pulled in a hiss of breath through her nose as she clearly recognized him. Her eyes went wide in fear, even hazed by illness as they were. He placed his gloved finger against her lower lip, silently begging her to be calm. To save her strength. She would need it all.

"I will not hurt you."

She would have to fight to survive. She would have to find her own strength to live. He had none to give her. For perhaps the others could lend themselves to bolster her in this middle-place between waking and dreams. But he? No. He could do no such thing. His power was meant to destroy, to kill, to corrupt. Not to sustain life.

Her expression was hazy as if she could not keep focus on him for long.

Ancients, I do not know what game you play. But do not let this one die.

Why? Why did he wish this? Why did he care? Curiosity or desire, perhaps? For even as she was now on the edge of death, the press of her body against his gave him pause. Made him deeply wish for the chance to do this once more when she was not struggling for breath.

For such a state was only enjoyable if *he* was the one who had put her in such a state. If *he* were the one holding the tether between her life and death. If it was his skill that kept her on the knife's edge.

This was very much out of his control. And there was little else that made him uncomfortable than loss of control. And so, he did the only thing he could think of to do; he urged her with words. "You must fight to survive. I can feel your heartbeat struggling, even from here. You must not let them take this from you."

"Please." The one word she mustered was little more than a delirious whimper. She was begging him. She was asking him for mercy—something he could not grant her. She pulled in a shuddering breath. "I can't..."

"Oh, but you must." Aon leaned his head down and rested his masked metal forehead against hers. He all but clung to her, wishing to impart anything he could to help her fight to keep her heart beating. He did not understand what had happened to her or what had placed her in such a state. But he knew it was far too unique to be a simple mishap. "Do not end this so soon. You are stronger than this, I can feel it. Fight. *Fight*, Lydia. You and I are not yet done."

And like that, she was gone. Slipping into the oblivion as she slipped back out of his dreams.

May she live. Please, may she live. Let her wake from what put her here.

May she be not the only one who may wake.

Aon reached out his power and grasped onto the thread that kept him only surface-deep into this fugue state of sleep. Oh, yes, it was a charming nothing that he slept until "fate" allowed him to wake.

It was a lie, as was all the rest of the pretense in this dying world.

Aon *never* surrendered control. Never. Not to Edu, and certainly not to the Ancients. He slept his hundred years as was decreed, only for that he enjoyed the peace of it.

But now, he very much had the need to wake.

Why? Why her? Why here?

A mystery worth solving. A body worth having. A soul he may find pleasure in knowing, at least briefly, before he dashed his little dream-thief's brains out upon the stone as he usually did with his playthings when he was done.

But he would never turn down the opportunity for diversion. And his newest potential toy was now hovering on the edge of death.

No. She is mine. That much is now quite clear. She is mine to destroy.

He yanked on the threads of power and felt the surge as he began to rise toward the surface of the waking world. But it would take time before he could arise.

He could only hope beyond hope that he would not be too late.

ELEVEN

Lyon could only pray to the Ancients that he was not a moment too late.

The impetuous, inquisitive young girl who had wandered from the caverns in search of answers had not risen from the pool. All had transpired as was the custom, until he perceived that a single heart's beat of time had stretched too long forward without her return.

Wading in, he quickly found her, lifeless and still just beneath the surface. Quickly, he scooped her up into his arms. She was limp. Carrying her to the platform, he placed her down upon the stone and knelt at her side.

What he saw struck him dumb—he stared, stunned, at what he beheld. There was no ink nor mask on her face. No scrawling, spiraling letters detailing, indecipherable as they may be, who she was to become or what role she may play in this world.

Nor was she corrupted. Her body had not twisted into one of the many species of creatures who called this place home. She was human.

Mortal.

This was impossible.

Grasping her wrist, he lifted her arm, rolling up the wet fabric of her thin coat to view the mark upon her forearm. It had been there not moments prior—the one labeling her as a chosen of the Ancients. It, too, inconceivably, was absent from her skin.

Gone.

What?

He jolted in surprise as the young girl convulsed violently with an unseen force, even as she was not awake to suffer through the pain that it must have caused.

The blood of the Ancients would not be contained in any vessel, not even within a body. Unconscious as she was, the liquid forced its way out of her lungs and her stomach. He could only roll her onto her side to aid the forcible exit of the ichor. It poured onto the polished stone, coursing from her lips and her nostrils indelicately before oozing back toward the pool to rejoin the whole.

When her body was free of the substance, he put his hand to her neck and felt for a pulse. But he had no time to register whether the poor thing was alive. As the last ounce of blood left her body, she gasped, her back arching and eyes shooting wide.

At least for the moment, she lived.

"Be still." He rested his hands on her shoulders, trying to keep her from injuring herself.

Caught in a wild panic, her hands grasped at him. She focused on him but for a moment, before bright blue eyes rolled back into her head. Once more, she was unconscious, slumping to the stone.

"What happened?" Maverick was the first to speak.

Lyon could merely shake his head at the doctor. There was no explanation he could provide for what had just transpired.

"Lyon, you idiot, what have you done?" The rage from Otoi

was instant. The corpulent little man in white looked down his literal beak at where he knelt upon the stones.

The insult did not trouble Lyon, nor was he concerned that any of those who heard the invective might pay it any mind. Otoi was the elder of Lyon's own house, but none assembled upon the platform held the obese man in any esteem, and for tremendous and rightful reasons.

Never was Otoi found without beads of sweat upon his waxen forehead, and this occasion was no different. His corpulent face scrunched in disgust as he glared down at where Lyon knelt.

"Otoi, begone," Elder Kamira snapped at the smaller man. The wild woman in the forest-green loincloth bore markings more than just those which the Pool of the Ancients had given her so long ago. She had seen fit to decorate herself of her own will, procuring some new piece of art each time she returned to Earth. Her braided hair jingled as she moved, the many beads and adornments tinkling together.

The little man flinched at her aggression before recoiling as she made a brief and stilted lunge in his direction. It was just enough to make Otoi leap back in fear. Otoi grumbled in frustration as Kamira laughed at his terror, huffed another insult under his breath, and turned to waddle back to the stairs leading to the crowd and the dozen of the chosen who still were to endure their Fall.

"Lydia!" someone screamed from the group of those being led from the room. A young man was trying to push his way forward, attempting desperately to reach the platform. Ah, yes —the other troublemaker, the one whom Lyon had rather inelegantly thrown through the gateway from Earth. "Lydia!" He was quickly shoved out of the room with the other chosen.

Lyon was given a brief moment to reflect on his own poor manners—he had never asked the girl her name in his previous dealings with her. So quick was he to dismiss the mortals in their brief lingering state between their world and Under.

Troublesome.

He had long since ceased to listen to Otoi's speech or the murmur from the crowd as he addressed those who came to watch. Lyon turned his attention back to the woman on the ground before him.

"Lyon." Kamira reached out to place a hand on his shoulder. It was a familiar gesture, and he did not shy away from the touch. He knew it well. They were mates, after all. "Is this... even possible? She bears no mark. It's *gone.*"

"I do not know." He shook his head. "Nowhere in the lore does it speak of anything such as this."

"It has never happened." Elder Ziza needn't speak loudly for her voice to carry, nor did she need to place much emphasis upon her words for them to be accepted as a pure and simple fact. The woman with eyes like ice carried herself as similarly as frozen water. "Not once, in all eras of Under."

Lyon looked up and saw the other elders and even King Edu had approached him and the young girl on the floor. Ziza, in her long blue dress and stark white hair, was gazing sightlessly with her empty, glasslike expression. Often, he was accused of being barren of all emotion. If that were so, Ziza was the void given flesh.

Edu moved forward and tilted his head to one side as if attempting to discern the girl's mystery by that method alone. Whatever the king was thinking, he could not share. Ylena, his empath, was not welcome upon the platform for the ceremony, so the mute king could not speak.

"This is nonsense," came the short, gruff voice of Navaa. The large man in the full black suit was standing toward the back of the small group, arms crossed over his expansive chest. His bald head and sharply carved mask gave him the appearance of a skull, one Lyon knew the other man delighted in quite adamantly. "Simply cast her in and try again."

Lyon held up the woman's arm, with the sleeve rolled up for him to see. "The mark of the chosen is gone from her. She is untethered to this world. Should we cast her in again, she will die."

"So be it." Navaa shrugged. "The Ancients made a mistake, and they're rectifying it now by taking her life."

"Do not blaspheme so." It seemed the only emotion that Ziza could still conjure was the vexation of a schoolteacher. "The Ancients saw fit to bring her here, and *their* priest saw fit to save her. I remind you, Navaa, you serve the will of your sleeping master. Lyon serves the will of our originators."

Maverick crouched down alongside Lyon, his hand now hovering at Lydia's neck. "Her pulse is faint. There is little I may do for a victim of drowning, but if we are to attempt to salvage her life, I will assist."

Lyon found the man's offer perplexing. Maverick was one to keep to himself and actively desired to tarry as little as possible in the affairs and events of Under. Perhaps the knowledge that what had just occurred before him was a singular event was enough to draw him from the reclusive shadows of solitude.

Or, perhaps, there was another reason to blame.

Ziza moved to stand beside Edu and did not bother to look up at him when she spoke. The woman was blind, after all. The two of them yet found a means to communicate, despite their respective limitations. "What is your order, our king?"

Would Edu command her death? Or attempt to save the poor thing, to understand the meaning behind this new mystery?

Edu let out a heavy breath, his massive shoulders lifting and falling with the exhale. He pointed one finger at the girl, then jerked it away from the pool and toward the entrance hall. The command was clear; take her away.

There was a surprising amount of relief in Lyon's heart. He gently scooped the unconscious Lydia into his arms and rose from his knees. Her head lolled against his shoulder like that of a sleeping child's.

He struggled to grasp in its enormity the whole of what had just transpired, or of what it might mean for their future. For thousands of years and since time immemorial, the blood of the Ancients had marked the souls of Earth and gathered them unto their own.

For thousands of years, they collected the mortals here, to cut them from their same cloth. To weave their threads into the fading tapestry of Under.

What meant it, then, to steal a human from the Earth, and do this? What were their intentions, that they should take a mortal child only to cast her away?

The Ancients had refused her.

Now... what would they do with her?

* * *

What a curious little thing.

Edu stood over the body of the young girl where she lay in the meager cot of the cathedral's lodgings. These chambers were meant for the weary pilgrim, not to serve as a makeshift infirmary, but it would do for the time being.

What mean you, Creators of Old? To take this girl from Earth, only to cast her away?

There was no doubt she had borne the mark of the chosen. There was no doubt she had been picked by the Ancients to join their world, to let her sin weave into their mighty world of the damned. He had felt the pull of the mark that called him to take her to Under where she now belonged. He had seen it for himself. So had many others.

Cast into the blood of the Ancients, she should have risen as her true self, as her inner soul demanded she continue into eternity. Instead, she carried no mark upon her face—indeed, no ink *anywhere.* Lyon had stripped the girl of her soaked clothing and redressed her in dry garb to keep her from catching a "cold," or whatever nonsense Maverick had warned. Mortals were such fragile things.

If Edu had once been mortal, those days were long since gone from his mind.

But in removing her clothes, Lyon had confirmed there was not a speck of ink upon her. Not even that which had labeled her as chosen.

At first, Edu thought perhaps it had been merely a trick of the Gods, some new evolution of their kind. A symbol of progress, not a mystery. Perhaps her soulmark was simply somewhere else. But she was clean.

A hand touched his arm. Ylena.

"What is it that lies there?" Her voice echoed in his mind. Ylena was blind, after all. It was the cost for her singular devotion to him.

No, it was more than that.

It was his sad attempt to create, in his jealous hunger, an effigy of that which he could not have. It was not her doing, nor her fault, that she had lost her sight and become his empath. But, such things could no longer be changed.

He shared with her his sight, even as she shared with him her voice.

Edu reached out a hand and gently let his palm trace down over Ylena's long, black hair. He had removed his armor and sent it away with his squires to be cleaned and cared for the moment the ceremony had come to an end. His armor was meant for moments of grandeur, not tromping around in the halls of this irritatingly barren and cold cathedral.

Her hair was soft beneath Edu's touch, and she smiled faintly as he stroked its surface. Ylena enjoyed his affection greatly, and he was loath to admit how long it had been since he had shown her any.

Empaths were curious creatures, by trade. They could communicate in silent words, yes, but most often they conveyed in memories or in feeling alone. Frequently, Ylena would speak to Edu in the sensation of a word if not the language placed upon them by one tongue or another. He could feel from her the ache of loneliness suddenly sated, the praise she paid to a tender touch from a loved one.

"As tender as a bull," Edu responded to her thought, chiding them both. While he could never take Ylena as his consort, she was bound to his soul in a way a wife would never be. It was a singular connection that made their souls barely indistinguishable.

"As gentle as you are capable," came her playful, rebuking reply.

"I do not know what has become of her." Edu finally answered his empath's question.

Ylena frowned. *"I fear for her safety. All will come for her, to exploit what she may be, or to end her life to prevent it."*

The girl had been cast away. She had no gifts, no power granted to her. She was merely human. What purpose could she serve, as anything other than a jest paid to them by the Ancients? Indeed, the other option—to kill her, before she might prove to be a threat—seemed the safer course of action.

"Would that be so tragic, if she were to die?" Edu tilted his head to the side as he watched the girl where she lay. His long hair fell in front of the eye of his mask as he did, but it did not trouble him. He was accustomed to it. *"Should she live?"*

"If you felt not the need to keep her alive, she would be dead.

You know in your heart that the Ancients have not done this without any cause. There is meaning in this. Take a breath before you seek to undo their will."

Ylena, his Ylena, always the voice of reason. The sounding calm to his raging sea.

Very well. Might the girl live through her ailment, he would allow it to continue. At least until he was given a good reason otherwise.

* * *

"Do not end this so soon," a voice purred close to her ear. Sharp and dangerous. "You are stronger than this, I can feel it. Fight. *Fight,* Lydia. You and I are not yet done."

The voice woke her up, but like her unconsciousness, it drifted away. Lydia clutched a pillow closer to her and let her fingers wind into the cotton fabric. It was rough and scratchy, honestly—but it was a pillow. And pillows meant sleeping, and sleeping was *terrific.*

Breathing hurt.

Not breathing hurt.

Everything hurt.

It felt like somebody had taken a bottle full of sand and made her swallow it all and then decided that "out the way it came" was more fun than through and made her hurl all of it back up. Or if somebody had wrapped a roll of sandpaper around a two-foot pipe cleaner and rammed it down her throat.

Cold water. That was what Lydia needed, suddenly and desperately.

It was the thing that finally forced her eyes open. Water. The thing that had started the problem was now the thing that she needed for comfort.

Huh.

I almost drowned.

Reaching out to the table next to her that she could barely put into focus, she tried to grasp the edge. She needed to move, to know where she was. She'd need to see, to know where she'd have to go, to get a glass of—

Her hand missed the table entirely and whiffed through the air weakly. It felt like a faster movement than it was, her hazy mind struggling to catch up. It was like the frames of a movie was out of sync with the audio.

A hand caught hers. Someone was sitting on the edge of the bed. Their voice was quiet, and it took a few words before Lydia caught any of them at all.

"... must be still," was all she managed to catch. The voice wasn't the same as the one who had woken her up. That voice had been deadly and sharp. This one was calming, soothing. Gentle.

She knew this voice. But her mind grasped at straws trying to recall who it was.

Lydia tried to speak, but what came out was a hacking cough. Once, as a kid, she had come down with food poisoning and had spent several days retching violently and destroying her throat. This brought that memory back.

The hand that had taken hers shifted away. It was helping her sit up. Barely. But enough. It placed a glass against her lips and was coaxing her gently to drink. Thank God. The water that touched her tongue was astonishing. It felt like heaven against the burning in her throat.

A few more sips and the world sank away from her once more. Her mission having been accomplished, her mind decided it didn't need her for anything else.

The nothingness was better.

* * *

"Master Edu has come to answer your call, Lady Ziza. He wonders what was so urgent to call him away from the cathedral." Ylena's hands were folded gently in front of herself as she addressed the Elder of Fate.

Ziza stood in the center of the great hall. It sat across the stretch of the city of Yej from the cathedral, and though it had not taken him much time to reach it, it was an inconvenience.

And Edu despised being inconvenienced.

More than that, however, Edu despised the city of Yej and wished nothing to do with it on a day-to-day basis. He *hated* its vehement adherence to society and "etiquette."

It was built to worship the false edification he loathed so profoundly. Platitudes and niceties and the desire to lay lace and gold upon that which deserved no such reverence.

They were a race of violence, death, and murder. They should not seek to rise above such things.

Ziza gestured upward, toward the grand orrery that represented the movements of their world. Her role was to interpret the actions of the magnificent sculpture, in the absence of her sleeping queen. "I thought perhaps our king would be interested to note the change for himself."

Casting his gaze up, Edu's brow furrowed behind his mask. Change, indeed. It barely resembled the structure he had seen only yesterday.

The metal rings had shifted drastically from one axis to another. Earth was clicking faster out of alignment with Under than it had been only hours before.

This changed the hunt for the marked from idle sport to a dire emergency. If their schedule had escalated, they would need to redouble their efforts to gather all those chosen to descend before the worlds passed out of phase.

"*Go,*" he commanded Ylena.

The empath bowed to Ziza and turned and left without another word. Ziza did not respond. While she had not seen the empath bow her head, it was not for that reason the elder of the House of Fate did not return the gesture.

Ziza could see all. Her dismissal of the polite gesture from Ylena was only because Ziza did not respond to very much of anything. Seeing all meant that she experienced all—and therefore, nothing much rose to the bar of being notable.

"It is not for that reason alone you should take note, my king." Her icy, placid voice filled the room easily, despite its light, whispering tone. She pointed a single finger and redirected his attention once more to the orrery above them.

The black orb. The impenetrable dark shape that represented the abhorrent warlock had changed its course as drastically as all the rest. It had been creeping unexpectedly closer—but now, it hovered dangerously near. This was an unnatural shift, even given how unpredictably erratic it could become. Edu had not seen movements this abrupt since during the days of the Great War that had sent their world inexorably into its descent toward destruction.

Edu's fists clenched tight at his sides.

He knew the warlock was going to rise early, but this meant Aon would rise in a matter of *days*. Turning, he stormed from the room, but he had not quite taken his leave before he heard Ziza's words echo from behind him in the expanse of the chamber.

"You know for what reason this has come to pass. More importantly—for *whom*."

* * *

Lydia was dreaming. There was a faint smell of old books and leather, and the feeling of soft, warm fabric under her cheek. She was lying on someone, her head tucked under their chin. There were arms around her. But she was already waking up, already trading the dream for the sensation of the cot beneath her. Both were true at once, and the illusion was losing ground and fading away.

The voice that cut into her haze was becoming familiar to her even as it grew distant. The man in the black metal mask— Aon. *"You lived? How wonderful. You are strong, my dear. You will need every ounce for what will surely come."*

It took Lydia several moments of blinking away the dream before she felt like she had a brain in her head again. Where she was, though, made no sense. It looked like she was in a jail cell of some kind. Bars were the first thing she noticed, backlit from the other side by a row of torches, tucked into rings on a dingy stone wall.

She was lying on a cot that felt like it had been stuffed with straw. It was lumpy underneath her back. Two of the walls of her cell were made of roughly hewn boulders. The other two walls were bars, creating a small, ten-foot-by-ten-foot box. She was in the corner of a much larger row of rooms that she couldn't quite see in the darkness.

It took her a long moment to realize she wasn't alone.

A figure sat in the cell with her on a rickety, thin-spoked chair, next to an equally pathetic-looking little table. The tiny, spindly-legged table sported a candle, providing the man the ability to read. Lyon, the Priest, had his head lowered, looking down at a book in his lap. In the dramatic and faint lighting, he resembled a painting. Or a portrait of a statue of a man reading, maybe.

"Two thousand years, and you haven't read them all?" Lydia coughed. But hey, she could talk. Weakly—but whatever—she'd succeeded. It hurt but not like before. Her first question really should have been "what the hell happened?" or "why am I in a jail cell?" But with the couple of days she'd been having, she knew the answers wouldn't help her understand much in the end.

Lyon looked up, and his serene face was caught in a

moment of surprise. He closed the book quietly and placed it onto the table. The expression was gone as fast as it had come. He stood and shifted to sit on the edge of her wooden cot. He was probably the one who had been at her side and given her water. Why did he care? Seriously, why?

"I fear I have read that one before, yes." He adjusted the pillow behind her back until she could rest against the rough stone wall. "But it has been long enough that I have forgotten the details. There is joy in it, still."

"I've done that." She smiled at him in thanks for helping her sit up. "And I'm not nearly your age, so I guess that's fair." There wasn't a point in questioning his age. Or any of what she was seeing. This was real—for better or worse.

Definitely worse.

He leaned down to the ground, and she followed his movements as he reached for a pitcher and a glass that was sitting on the floor next to the cot. He poured water into the glass, set the pitcher back down, and straightened, holding the glass out to her. Every movement he made was measured and careful, every gesture with purpose. Of all the people she'd met here so far, he felt *ancient.*

Lyon helped her as she held the glass with both hands. It wasn't until she nodded to say she was pretty sure she wasn't going to dump it all over herself that he let go, though he kept his hand lingering nearby, in case her theory proved to be wrong. She raised the glass carefully to her lips and took a sip. Her hands felt weak, but she managed. Seemingly content with that level of success, he lowered his hand to his lap.

"Was that normal?" Lydia stopped to cough for a moment before resuming. "What the hell happened?" Gary had come out of the pond looking a little wobbly but none the worse for wear. Everyone else had walked themselves out, even if they emerged with more legs than when they went in. It didn't take a genius to realize what happened to her hadn't followed the pattern.

"It was certainly not normal." Lyon's face creased for a moment in an expression she could not quite understand, before smoothing back to the visage of a statue. "We do not know what transpired."

"You don't know."

He paused, seeming unsure of what to say. "When you entered the pool, you did not resurface. Instead of emerging as one of us, you nearly drowned. You have no marks upon you, nor have you been changed in form. You remain human."

Lydia tried to resist the urge to tell him how wonderful that was. Judging by the way Lyon said it, the topic was dire. To her, it meant she still had some strange, fleeting hope of going back to her normal world with her normal life. Well, except for one thing that popped into her head like the proverbial light bulb. "What happened to Nick?"

"We ceased the ceremony immediately after your ordeal. For now, the others wait in the chamber. Nick is unharmed."

Looking down at her arm, she saw that the symbol that had appeared on her right forearm was gone. "Does this mean I get to go home? Please tell me this means I get to go home." Hope bubbled up in her.

And was popped a second later.

He placed his hand upon her wrist as he spoke as if to soften the blow. "I would not recommend you foster much thought toward such things. It is for Master Edu to decide. To be frank, it is highly unlikely. He has called a council to determine your fate. They meet on the morrow to decide if you should live or die."

"*What?*" Lydia coughed. She wasn't ready to shout yet. "I'm no threat, I'm still human! Look at me. That stupid lake thing almost killed me. That doesn't make any sense."

"You may still be a threat. Though you appear to have no

power, you are... unnatural." He sighed. It was obvious he hated delivering the news, but this all seemed to be his duty. "We do not think you play a willing part in this, for what it may be worth to you."

Lydia couldn't help it. She just started laughing, despite how raspy and painful it was. The priest blinked, his brow furrowing slightly at her reaction. She had to stop after a moment to cough. She took another sip of water before trying to explain why she had burst out laughing.

She had the kind of morbid sense of humor that found the worst things funny at the worst possible times. "Sorry, I'm just reflecting on how typically awful my luck is. Only I would wind up being triple-screwed."

"I do not understand."

"First, your weird mask-wearing monster cult gives me a mark. Great. I get chased around by some asshole in a suit of armor and abducted. Great. Then you put me in your weird blood puddle, and then it decides to change its mind? Now you're telling me Edu might kill me anyway, for shit I had nothing to do with." Lydia shut her eyes, her anger and humor threatening to fade into fear and grief. Lydia let out a long, tired sigh.

"I am very sorry."

"Where the hell am I now? Not that it matters, really, I guess."

"You are in Edu's keep, some miles away from the cathedral in which you woke. You are contained in this cell to protect you from others who may not be so inclined to wait for an official verdict."

"You said he was going to kill me."

"I said there was a possibility. The matter is still very much up for debate."

"He's locked me up to protect me so that he can then decide *whether or not* to kill me?"

"Yes."

"Fuck." Lydia sighed heavily. The big suit of armor was a king, and he could do what he wanted. In some ass-backward way, locking her up kept her in one place. It kept people from getting in, just as much as it kept her from wandering off. Whatever.

He rested his hand on her shoulder and tried his best to console her. "If he wanted you dead, he would have done so without hesitation. I believe he wishes to understand what has transpired."

"And *then* he might kill me."

"Yes."

"You're not helping."

When she looked back at him, he had a faint, barely-there smile on his face. At least he seemed to understand that her frustration was not aimed at him. He squeezed her shoulder gently. It was about then she realized she wasn't wearing her regular clothes.

Instead, she was dressed in a long, gray cotton dress with laces up the front, keeping the panels together. "What the hell am I wearing?"

"I had to change your clothing."

"*Dude!*"

He likely didn't understand the definition of a word so entirely out of his own time. But since Lydia said it in the tone of someone who just got cut in line at the grocery store, he at least seemed to catch her indignant meaning.

"You were soaked to the bone. Maverick rightly recommended we not leave you in such a state, lest you catch ill. I apologize."

"Yeah, great. Spare my life before you *kill me*." Lydia sighed and put her hand over her face. What was an insult added to injury, anyway? She'd nearly died. They did what they had to do to keep her alive so they could decide whether to kill her anyway. "It's fine. Sorry. Thanks."

Lyon laughed once, nearly silently through his nose. "You are welcome." He stood from the cot after a moment and moved to gather his book from the table. "You should rest. Lord Edu is not a patient man, and I expect matters will progress in short order."

"At least I won't be bored for long." Humor was the best armor she had at the moment.

His expression was soft, a mix of amusement and sympathy, as he opened the cell door and stepped outside of it, twisting the large key and engaging the mechanism with a heavy clunk. "For what little it is worth, I have faith in the workings of the Ancients. I believe you belong here, and we will be a greater whole for your part in it."

It was a surprising compliment. Something about the way he said it deflated any lingering annoyance at the way she'd been treated. He was expressing that he saw some value in her. That wasn't something Lydia heard often. It left her agog for a beat, and he turned to walk away.

Before Lyon began moving, she finally answered. "It means a lot. Thank you."

Lyon turned his head to glance at her, ice blue eyes catching the torchlight, and a sad smile graced his features as he walked down a stone hallway and out of sight.

Once he was gone, she scooted back down onto the bed and lay back on the pillow. If the other cells contained other unhappy prisoners of King Edu, she didn't have the strength of will to find out right now. He'd recommended she sleep, and there was a statement she didn't feel like arguing.

At least in her mind, Lydia was safe.

At least she thought she was.

In her dream, the corpse from the lab was after her once more, chasing her through the hallways of her workplace. She tore around corners that weren't there before, racing through the nonsensical landscape of her dreaming mind.

"Help!" she cried, just as she had during the real event. "Somebody, *help!*"

The creature was hunting her. It didn't matter that the places she was running through shouldn't connect in the waking world. She could hear the monster, snarling and screeching at her, calling out for her blood. Crying out to end her life.

Desperately, she rounded a corner and slammed full tilt into someone. They took a step back with the impact before managing to stop her. A pair of hands settled onto her shoulders, one gloved, one clawed. At that moment, the streets of Boston dissolved. She was no longer running from a monster—

She had run into the grasp of one.

A dark voice purred down to her, amused. "*You called?*"

TWELVE

This didn't feel like a dream.

Or at least, not a normal one.

Not this shit again.

Lydia was drowning. Liquid was filling her lungs, and she couldn't breathe. She was beneath the surface of the water, looking up at the rippling reflection of a figure standing over her. She felt her heart seize in her chest, felt the fear course through her like electricity. She felt helpless and frozen in time.

"I heard your cries, calling to me through the darkness."

The voice was the same as the one in all her recent dreams.

"Why do you fear the water? Why have you dreamt this suffering for yourself?"

Sharp and dark like a knife in the shadows.

"As delightful as this may be to watch, it does make conversation rather dull."

The figure she could barely see through the liquid moved closer as if crouching to look down at her through the surface of a frozen lake. He reached down, a black-gloved hand appearing before her. Palm up, fingers stretched, offering.

Anything to get out of the water.

Grasping his hand, he took hers in return. When he tugged, she was no longer in the water. She was standing in the middle of... well, nowhere. Stretching on in all directions was emptiness, the ground reflective like black glass. The shine on the floor faded to darkness and left everything else utterly empty.

Except for the man standing in front of her. Clothed entirely in black, the only reason he stood out from the darkness around him was that there still seemed to be a source of pale light coming from somewhere, separating him from the shadows.

Watching him for a moment, she wondered if he was going to leap at her and tear her to pieces. But the only movement he made was to clasp his hands behind his back, seemingly content to give her a moment to gather her wits.

She had vague memories of fever-like dreams after drowning, but she wasn't quite sure how much of that was real or simply a product of her own mind. Here, there was a fifty-fifty shot.

"I'm still dreaming?" she finally asked.

"Yes." Aon sighed. "Regretfully. However." He took a step toward her, his voice suddenly turning into a dark, dusky rumble. "Now I am strong enough to take control of our little... rendezvous." He took another step. She took one away from him in turn.

He chuckled. "I see." With that, he vanished, blinked out of existence in front of her as if he had never been there. Before she could even whirl around to see where he might have gone, an arm snaked around her waist from behind and yanked her abruptly against his chest. The smell of old books, of leather and dust, the scent of decaying paper was all around him like a strange cologne.

"Where do you think you may run, here in this world I control?" He would have sounded playful if he hadn't just grabbed her.

The tips of the sharp claws of his gauntlet were resting against her throat and close under her jaw. They felt like the points of knives. As he applied the slightest pressure, it forced her to tilt her head back and against his chest where it met his shoulder. It was that or risk being sliced open. Both her hands flew to grab at his wrist, trying to yank his hand away from her. But it was hopeless. She could barely budge him.

The touch of cold metal against her face brushed against her, and she realized his head was close to hers, almost nuzzling in toward her neck and her cheek. He made a low noise in his throat, and the arm around her waist pulled her tighter against him. "You are quite the lovely one, aren't you? Such fire I can sense within you. Tell me, my dear—as I have had to focus on other things as of late." His voice was a low, pleased rumble that dropped in tone as he lowered his volume. "How many times has that great dunderhead had his way with you already?"

"What?" She somehow took shelter in her indignancy at his question. She made sure not to open her mouth too far—or press herself into the dangerously stinging tips of his clawed gauntlet. "Dude, I've—I nearly drowned."

"Hmm?" He loosened his grip on her slightly and pulled his head back. "Edu has not taken your body yet? Surely, you jest. The oaf cannot keep his paws off anyone."

"What the *fuck* are you talking about?" Lydia yanked on his hand again. "Let me go. *Now*."

"At least you have finally found your spine." He released the grasp on her neck obediently. For a moment, she thought she was free of him, but no such luck. He let her only turn around in his arm before squeezing her back against him, and now she was face to face with him, her body pressed against his.

Lydia placed her palms against his chest and tried to push away but only managed to lean herself back a few inches. Before she could speak, his gauntleted hand was on her again, this time carefully taking her chin between his thumb and fingers and turning her head slowly left then right as if inspecting her. He didn't need to press hard for her to obey, as the points of his claws were needle sharp.

He was looking for a soulmark, she realized. The thing she should have but didn't. "What a marvel—I cannot help but think it was a figment of my shattered mind." He hummed. "Perhaps whatever nearly took your life saved you from such an insufferable event as being coerced into sleeping with that overgrown man-child. I suppose even he would not lower himself to sleeping with an unconscious, injured woman. Though, perhaps I am wrong. What to do with you, I wonder?"

Lydia couldn't respond with his knife-edge claws digging into her skin. But Aon didn't seem concerned. Instantly, the man struck her as someone who enjoyed the sound of his own voice. He was asking himself the questions, not her. Aon let out a low, thoughtful sound and leaned in closer. His mask, though featureless and black as obsidian, was unnerving and eerie. It sent chills up her spine.

"Edu will likely sentence you to death. Simply because is, in fact, deeply paranoid that you might represent change."

Aon released the grasp on her just barely, running the tip of his pointer finger along her temple, stroking her hair back behind her ear as if to get a closer look. The feeling of the sharp line being drawn caused her skin to break out in goosebumps.

"What a wonderful little mystery! Thrown away by the Ancients who chose you to join us. You are a threat to the natural order of things. How utterly charming. Yes, Edu will seek your head on a pike." He traced his claws around behind her ear, making her shiver. Aon let out another low chuckle in his throat at her reaction and leaned in closer. If he were not wearing a mask, she would fear he might move to kiss her. "How I will delight in unraveling you."

The dangerous threat and even more confusing sexuality that dripped from his voice was enough to make Lydia finally risk pulling back away from his nails. "Stop!" she said in a small squeak.

"Why?"

That jammed her thoughts and brought her to a straight, full stop. Why? "Because this isn't..." She trailed off, shocked that anybody would question why you weren't supposed to act like this.

"Yes? Isn't what?" Aon prodded, a playful, mischievous tone to his voice.

"I don't know—It isn't..." She grasped wildly at words until she found the first one and yanked it from the Rolodex, accuracy be damned. "It isn't polite." How was this her problem to figure out?

"Well! Do forgive me." Aon laughed. It was as sharp and dangerous as the points of his clawed hand. Vincent Price would have been proud.

Still, he let her go and took a step back from her, his hands held out at his sides. Theatrically, he took another small step back, and with a flourish, folded a hand in front of him and another at his back. Long tendrils of black hair fell forward as he bowed low.

"My dearest lady, allow me to introduce myself. You know my name, yet you do not know with whom you have parlayed with so much as of late. I am Aon, King of the House of Shadows. High Lord of Warlocks, and—if you are to ask any others —the paramount madman and sadist in Under." Sarcasm was layered so thickly on his words, they could've been a cake. "How honored I am to finally formally make your acquaintance, Miss *Lydia*." He nearly hissed the last word and lifted his head to glance at her, even as he didn't straighten from his bow. "Does this better suit your sense of etiquette?"

If there was one thing in the world she couldn't stand, it was being mocked. Her instant anger shoved all the fear away into a corner and replaced it with fury as quickly as the toll of a bell. She had been chased, threatened, and nearly killed. Now, she was probably going to die anyway! The last thing she was going to do was be insulted by some freak in a mask. "Okay, *look,* you asshole—"

In the blink of an eye, he disappeared again. Lydia stammered to a stop and turned, terrified of where he might have gone. Her anger popped like a bubble. He had called her bluff without having to do anything.

"Careful, my dear..." Aon purred from the darkness. "I am not one to be trifled with. I would not so casually insult a king."

"I thought Edu was king."

A growl of frustration floated from nowhere. "Edu is *a* king. Hardly the only one to rule this world. I am equal in rank to him, and far greater in all other matters, I assure you."

"Uh-huh." Lydia turned about slowly, hopelessly looking for him. "You weren't at the Ceremony of the Fall, or whatever you weirdos call it."

"I lie in my crypt, as you saw. Asleep, but not for long. I plan to intervene in these affairs. Therefore, I would be far more prudent with your words before you decide to levy invectives in my direction. You very well may be doing so in person before long."

"I'm having a really rough couple of days, all right? I'm sorry. But I don't need to be insulted on top of everything. It's bad enough that I get chased, hunted, and nearly drown. You're haunting my dreams, and now I'm locked in a goddamn cell, and—"

"What?"

The voice came from directly behind her, and she screamed and whirled around. She likely would have tripped over her own legs and fallen if Aon hadn't interceded. He cackled and caught her around the waist with an arm, snaking it around her and pulling her up against him.

"Fuck—knock it off!" Lydia shoved her hands against his

chest, trying to break away from him, but he was immovable. When his clawed and metal hand went to her throat, she froze. He seemed content to settle his hand against the crook of her neck where it met her shoulder. "We do not have time. Explain yourself. You are a prisoner? Whose?"

"Edu's," Lydia peeped out.

Aon snarled deep in his throat, and his grasp on her tightened. "And what, precisely, does that mountainous waste of flesh intend to do with you?"

Lydia swallowed thickly. "I don't know."

"Does he know we are already acquainted?"

"N-no."

He honestly sounded surprised. "You listened to me? Good. Then heed my words again, my dear. Edu will seek your death. One way or another. Be sure of it."

"But I have nothing to do with any of this."

"It matters not. Trust me."

"Lyon said some people are going to have a meeting to decide what to do with me. He said it wasn't decided yet."

"Lyon is a compassionate fool who wished to foster in you some semblance of false hope. Edu will seek to take your life within the week, I am certain. No one has ever returned from the Pool of the Ancients unchanged. You are a threat to the natural order of our world. And if he believes I have anything to do with your misfortune, he will murder you in a heartbeat to spare this world whatever plot he thinks I have concocted. I needn't remind you of the continued importance of not speaking of our conversations." He tightened his hand just a bit for good measure before relaxing.

That raised a really good question. "*Do* you have anything to do with this?"

"I am flattered." Aon chuckled. "But, sadly, no. I fear you will pay the price, regardless. Tell me, do you wish to die?"

"No." Lydia didn't hesitate.

"Choosing death will spare you much torment and suffering. Death at his hands will be quick. You are a mortal in a world of monsters who hunger to see things like you twisted, broken, and consumed."

"Does that include you?"

Aon chuckled again, pleased with her jab. "Oh, very much *yes*. You cannot begin to fathom what I wish to see done to you." The insinuation in his voice dripped like hot wax, and she tried once more to recoil from him, desperately hoping to shrink away.

The clawed hand at her shoulder slipped around her throat and tightened. Aon snapped from one mood to another without warning. One second, he was having a conversation with her. The next, he was digging the points of his claws into the sides of her throat, bringing tears to her eyes as it stung dangerously and threatened to break the surface. The man was quicksilver.

"You may count me first and foremost on that list, my darling. So, tell me..." He tilted her head back, the claws now digging in a little harder. Lydia cried out as she felt them pierce her skin, but here in the dream, at least she knew it wasn't real. But it didn't stop it from feeling real. "Knowing that creatures such as I wait for you, do you change your mind? Do you now wish your life to end?"

"No—" Lydia insisted through the fear.

"Even knowing I will come for you?"

"I don't want to die."

"Good girl."

Her mind went white as his claws dug deep into her throat.

* * *

Jolting awake, Lydia swore under her breath. She'd woken up to the sound of harshly squeaking metal, of rust on rust. *Oh, Christ.*

Coming out of her nightmare, she sat up and rubbed her hands over her face. Her heart was pounding a mile a minute, and the sudden state change between being murdered by Aon and sitting in a cell made her a little woozy. For a second or two, she forgot where she was and what was happening.

This wasn't her bed.

The reality of the situation smashed back in an instant and she swore quietly again.

The noise had been the door to her cell opening, and a man was putting a tray of food on the rickety little table Lyon had been using previously. The man had a large red swatch of a spiral along his left jawline and cheek.

He barely glanced at her before he exited the cell, shut the door, locked it, and left. Lydia swung her legs off the edge of the bed and put her head in her hands.

"Bad dream?"

She looked up at the unexpected voice. In the cell next to her was a young woman leaning against the wall, a tray in her hands. The first thing she noticed was the woman's red hair, that kind that some people would kill for, and others would love to get rid of. It was a mop of tight natural curls that seemed almost impenetrable around her face. It was pulled back in a sloppy ponytail at the back of her head, with plenty of the red spirals left to escape around her freckled, pale face.

The girl had one of those faces that made her look younger than she probably was. She had a bright purple soulmark on her cheek just under her right eye. It was about the size of a half dollar and didn't detract from her beauty. The girl was stunning, in that "good ol' American countryside" kind of way. Something about her just spoke of cornfields and cows to Lydia. Her eyes were a dark tone of yellow, almost amber. Something about the purple marks made their eyes go yellow. Maverick, Gary, and now this girl. Weird.

"Yeah." It felt stupid to admit she was having a nightmare, but fuck if she didn't have a good excuse.

"Sounded like a nasty one." The girl was already picking at the food on the tray in her lap. Oh, yeah, she was a country girl, judging by the accent. Somewhere in the Midwest, a land that was as foreign to Lydia as Norway, if she were honest.

"Lotsa mumbling." The girl let out a noise that indicated she remembered her manners and laughed. "Sorry! Always getting away from myself. I'm Evelyn." She stuck her hand through the bars from her neighboring cell. "But everyone calls me Evie." Her face was brimming with a show-stopping smile that was gorgeous and innocent at the same time. "Nice ta'meetcha!"

Something was so gosh darn bubbly about the girl—who was also locked in a jail cell—that was infectious. Smiling, Lydia stood from the cot and moved closer to shake her hand. "Lydia. Or Lyd, either work. And... you too."

"Pleasure."

How could someone be so chipper in such a dire situation? She'd kill for an ounce of that level of optimism. It just didn't come naturally to her, no matter how hard she tried.

Evie gave her hand a hard squeeze and a firm shake and was still grinning as they mutually let go. "Well, better get to that dinner of yours before it goes cold. It ain't too good when it's warm, and it sure ain't any better when it's not."

"Adorable" was the word that came to mind for Evie. Lydia smiled at her and went to get her tray of food. She could have sat on her cot to eat, but instead, she found herself sitting opposite the bars from Evie, leaning up against the same wall and mimicking the girl's pose, with the tray in her lap.

The redhead was still smiling broadly. She dropped her

voice, mimicking the sound of a man, and gruffed, "So, what're you in for, bub?"

Lydia laughed. Shit, she needed a laugh today. It sent her off in a peal of laughter that was so wonderfully cathartic. She let it trail off and found the girl was smiling at her, broad-faced and proud of her accomplishment.

"I'm here because, apparently, 'the Ancients' or whatever they are can't make up their goddamn minds." Yep, she was bitter. And she wasn't going to feel bad about it at all.

Evie grinned. "I heard. I just hadda ask, anyway. Only get to make that joke a few times, y'know? The Priest was sittin' here for quite a while, fussing over you, wonderin' if you were gonna cash in your chips." She let out a whuf and stuffed a piece of bread in her mouth, chewing on it even as she spoke, making everything afterward come out muffled. "Never seen him worried before."

"Does this place only have one priest? Everybody calls him 'the' Priest."

"Only one that matters, only one worth the title," Evie responded with a shrug. "Don't pinch the details." She shifted excitedly, nudging closer to the bars. "You got marked, you got fetched, you got thrown in, and then..."

"Nearly drowned." The dress she was wearing had short sleeves, and when she looked down at her forearms, there was no mark on either arm. Well, one had a faint light patch where the healed skin was left from her home surgery attempt. Maverick did a good work, she had to admit. "Now Edu has me locked up here. He thinks I'm a threat."

"Psh, Edu may be a helluva baby grand, but that fella doesn't think much before he acts. Stuck you in here until he could work somethin' out." Evie ripped off a chunk of bread again and shoved it into her mouth.

"Where're you from originally?" The smile she wore refused

to leave when talking to Evie. That was fine by her, she needed it. Poking around at the tray, she quickly found the fruit and a few pieces of cheese more interesting than the hunk of bread and the small bowl of... some brown stew.

"Montana." Evie's tone never flinched from its brightness. "You also got to learn to ask *when,* bunny."

"Fair." Shaking her head, she chewed on a piece of cheese, realizing how hungry she was. "When're you from, Evie from Montana?"

"When I got snatched?" Evie leaned back on the stone wall and looked up at the ceiling thoughtfully. "It was nineteen twenty-two."

"Follow up." Lydia found the girl easy to talk to. She had a casual, easy flair, and Lydia was happy to have someone that wasn't... well, Evie wasn't human. The mark on her face and yellow eyes were clear indications. But she wasn't a stone visage like the Priest. Or extremely punchable like Tim. "What're you doing in here?"

Evie took in a big breath and let it out in a long, loud sigh. "I ain't so bright. I tried to kill somebody. See, to not have a mask makes you a servant. You serve everybody. The... monsters too." Evie shook her head. "I took it until I couldn't take it no more, I guess."

Whatever Evie was alluding to... wasn't pleasant. "How do you serve a monster?" Everybody in Under seemed *extremely* horny. *Please don't be sex, please don't be—*

"You feed them."

There was such weight behind those three words that Lydia decided to sort out in silence what she meant. When it finally dawned on her, the result sent a cold chill down her back.

Oh.

They couldn't die. Not by violence, anyway. Which meant servants were required to... to feed the monsters. Judging by the look on her face, she meant it in the worst way possible. Not "go get the dog chow." Evie was saying she *was* the dog chow. Repeatedly.

Was that better or worse than it being a sexy thing? She honestly didn't know. Maybe this class system of theirs wasn't a benign one. It didn't really come as a surprise, to be honest.

"So, I got sick of it. Refused to do it. Was told either to shut up and do my duty or I'd serve the monsters differently, if you catch my drift."

Well, that answered that. "You tried to break free. I'd have done the same."

"Yup. I figured, useless dewdropper boss of mine, it'd be easy to get the jump on 'im. I went to cut off his mark, and I just couldn't do it. Never been much of an iron stomach." She set her tray aside on the ground next to her. "Thought I had more gumption than I did."

"Why would you cut his mark off?"

"The ones on our face, they're important. You can't kill somebody unless you take it off 'em first. Burn it, cut it, doesn't matter. Then they can die." Evie shrugged. "Couldn't tell ya why. But otherwise, we just keep comin' back."

"That sucks."

Evie laughed. "Only for us servants. To everybody else, it's a sport."

"That's why it sucks." Lydia leaned back on the wall and decided to try dipping a piece of bread into the brown stew and taking a bite out of it. It wasn't awful, but it wasn't great either. It tasted a lot of flour and some over-boiled meat.

Wait...

"What's the meat in this stew?" she asked Evie slowly, terrified of the answer as the question dawned on her slowly, connecting their previous conversation to this one. *Oh, please, don't let it be Soylent Green.*

Evie cracked up at that, howling in laughter and slapping

the floor next to her in great excitement. "Oh, boy! The look on your face! I should tell you it's servant and really pull your leg." Finally, she managed to calm down enough to explain, wiping tears from her eyes. "It ain't a person. It's from one of those monsters you probably saw come out of the lake. We eat them, they eat us. I just got sick of it being my only job around here."

"But the monsters also used to be people."

Evie sighed sympathetically and leaned up against the bars. "Yup. Bunny, welcome to Under."

They sat in silence for a long time, and Lydia shook her head, feeling deflated and hopeless again. She didn't know why she felt the need to confess to Evie how she was feeling. It was rare that Lydia made a fast friend. Maybe it was the fact that they were stuck in here together or the bright smile on Evie's face that seemed to never waver for long, but she wanted to trust her.

"This is all a nightmare. A total, fucked up nightmare. I just want to go home. But I learn that Edu'll probably kill me because of something that isn't my fault. It's bad enough that I have that asshole in black haunting my dreams and—"

Shit.

She wasn't supposed to say anything.

"Huh?" Evie turned to look at her, bright yellowy-amber eyes blinking in curiosity. "Who's in your dreams?"

Lydia paused before speaking again, her voice low. "Can I trust you?"

"Of course, bunny."

"Nobody can know."

"An' who'm I gonna tell?"

"He said if they don't already want me dead, they will when they learn he's... somehow magically screwing around in my head."

"Aon..." The way Evie said the name, it was like she was

afraid she'd summon the man with the word alone. "It's him, isn't it?"

"How did you know?"

Evie ignored her question and leaned into the bars. "What has Aon been doing in your dreams? All the details!"

"He keeps showing up every damn time I fall asleep or pass out. And I think he was watching me on Earth. Fucking creep." Putting the tray aside, she pulled her knees up toward her chest and rested her arms on them. "Harassing me or threatening me, last time he said he's getting stronger and—"

"Oh, no..." Evie moaned and sank backward. Apparently, all the details weren't needed. "Oh, no. Oh, this is no good."

"What?"

"That means he's waking up." She sat back and put her head in her hands. "I'm doomed. *We're* doomed!"

"Whoa, whoa, slow down." Lydia reached through the bars and put her hand on the girl's thin shoulder. "Is he that much worse?"

"You have no idea! If Aon's rising, then Edu and he will have to trade places, and Aon will be in charge. Oh, no... no, no, no!" She cried into her hands.

"Why is this so awful?" Lydia had met Edu and Aon now, and both seemed like complete jackasses. Why was one so much worse than the other?

"Edu was just going to execute me." Evie sniffled and wiped her nose. "Aon... he prefers to torture the prisoners. Bunny, what gets sent back out of his cells ain't the same as what goes in. He's a sadist. He's insane!"

"Torture? Like... what?"

"He peels people's skin off in sheets. He bleeds them dry, again and again and again. He puts people up to their necks in boiling water and melts their flesh off their bones. He—"

"Stop, stop," Lydia interrupted, her stomach twisting. That was who was in her dreams. That was who was coming after her. *That's what he's going to do to me. He said it himself.* "I'm sorry I asked."

"Edu's a lotta things, but he ain't cruel. Aon... the only thing he loves in this world is causing pain. I'm a prisoner. So're you. Don't you get it?"

Leaning back against the wall, she tried to let it settle over her. Aon said others would describe him as the paramount madman and sadist in Under. And he was right. Glancing over at Evie, she considered the fact that she wasn't alone now. If Edu didn't kill her first, something told her she still wouldn't make it very long.

And if she was going to get out of this prison, she'd need Evie's help. A terrible plan started to form in her mind. "Evie? There's one more thing you should know."

"Yeah?" She wiped her eyes, swiping away her tears.

"Aon isn't just waking up. He's waking up... because of *me.*"

* * *

Aon heard Lydia's words echo through his mind.

"He's waking up... because of me."

The fear in her words was unmistakable. The terror. The *disgust.* Yes. Oh, yes. Dear, sweet, wonderful little mystery. *Come to loathe me like all the rest—I will delight in it as I unwrap you, layer by layer, until you are not but sinew and bone.*

How he delighted in their conversations thus far. The way she blushed—blushed!—at his nearness and his touch. The way he could feel her pulse quicken beneath his hand as he hinted at just what kind of heights and depths he could show her.

Poor little thing. Lost and afraid.

But he could not dally. He must wake—and wake quickly. He did not trust the council to see value in Lydia's life. Nor did he trust Edu not to overrule their decision if they did. No, the hotheaded bastard would attempt to murder Lydia, no matter what the elders voted.

If he did not hurry, it would be too late for her.

He would never let Edu harm her. No—that pleasure would be his and his alone.

She was *his*.

THIRTEEN

"It is too soon. It cannot be!"

"You have seen the movements yourself. You know it to be true."

"But he rises early."

"But why? Why now?"

"It is because of the girl."

"That is a safe presumption, yes."

"If that is true, then it foretells miserable days for us all, when that *arsehole* returns."

"Mind yourself, Kamira. As Master Aon rises soon, you may mark your words."

"Mark your own, Navaa. Your master and I know each other quite well. My disdain for his methods and his demeanor is no news to him."

Edu slammed his fist onto the tabletop, sending the goblets atop the wood surface rattling and rolling about. Otoi had to grab his goblet with both hands to keep it from toppling over. Edu had enough of their bickering, their rumble and noise. All six of them sat around the table, with Edu at the head, Ylena standing to the side behind his massive, rough-hewn wood chair.

Her hands were clasped neatly in front of her as she waited for the room to fall silent. "Master Edu agrees that this timing is conspicuous enough to render a coincidence unlikely. Somehow, the girl's unique condition has awoken Aon, despite it barely being thirty years into his sleep."

"What do you think he will do with her?" Maverick asked.

"Dissect her and add her to his collection, I expect." Kamira raised her glass to her lips, sipping the mix of blood and wine those whose masks did not cover their mouths could imbibe. Indeed, he was the only one who could not share in it. It was an unfortunate side effect of his seat of power. If he wished to be drunk, he must do so alone. With Aon rising from his crypt in short order, he felt the overwhelming need to release tension in any way he could.

"Do not presume to speak for my Master." Navaa shot Kamira a look that could wither a plant.

"Oh? And what do *you* believe he may do with the girl?" Kamira snorted. "Bake her a cake? Make her comfortable? Please, he would dice her organs out upon the slab to see what secrets she might hold, and you know it."

"She is the first known to have been rejected by the Ancients." Maverick shook his head. "Killing her would end her mystery immediately. I do not feel that Aon, mad as he may be, would be so... rash."

Navaa sneered at Kamira, who could only glare at the studious gentleman in purple for interceding in her argument with Navaa. Maverick shrugged and took a sip of his own glass, unflinching in the face of Kamira's anger. The Elder of Moons was often angry. It was not an unusual condition for any of them to navigate.

"Aon has just as much say in her fate as any of us." Navaa leaned back in his chair. The Elder of the House of Shadows would step down as soon as his master rose. And in turn, Edu would return to his own crypt beneath his keep. Oanr, his second in command, would then rule for the Flame.

Such was the treaty they had struck at the end of the war that had cost them all so very much.

But for Aon to rise early, what might it mean for the mystery of the girl who had been rejected by the Ancients? Could Edu allow himself to sink into over a century of sleep with such a threat?

Perhaps the girl was a freakish mistake. She may be nothing, a fruit fly to creatures like them. Or something could dwell in her, some deep reasoning that could spell doom for all of them if the key to such things fell to Aon's control.

"Master Edu reminds you that Aon has not yet risen. Edu is still king. Therefore, it is for the council to decide what to do with the girl."

"What are our options?" Kamira lifted a hand to count off on her fingers. "Kill her. Release her to Earth. Throw her back to the Ancients for a second try. Keep her as a human pet." Kamira shrugged. "I care not which."

"Be wary," Ziza warned. "The Ancients have chosen this path for her for a reason. Death may be imprudent."

"Do you know that for certain?" Maverick peered at the woman in blue curiously.

"I have had no visions on the matter, no. But I can feel their hand working heavily in these matters." Ziza shut her pure white eyes as if listening to unheard music.

"Keep her alive until Aon wakes." Navaa tapped the table with his pointer finger. "Convene again when a king with more knowledge may provide his opinion on her fate."

Edu growled low in his throat, wordlessly warning the Regent of the House of Shadows to watch his tongue, lest he wind up without one in short order. Edu rattled off in his mind a colorful description regarding precisely where into Navaa's anatomy he was going to install the man's head if he were not silent.

"I will opt not to voice that, my king," Ylena chided him silently.

Even Navaa shrank back in his chair at Edu's change in posture. Some things could be conveyed without words.

"I don't think we should kill the girl." Otoi rubbed his hand across his upper lip. "Seems a waste. She's the first damn interesting thing to come out of that pond in a long time. The Ancients put her here. I say we keep her and watch her."

"You spoke with the girl." Kamira glared at Maverick. "What say you?"

"I did, but briefly. Hardly long enough to discern any salient details. Lydia has spirit, conviction." He paused thoughtfully. "Will."

"We learned that when she buried a bullet into Edu's skull." Navaa sneered.

Edu rose from his chair, glaring a hole through Navaa where he sat.

The man in black raised his hands in surrender. "No offense, my king. Any of us would have been taken off guard. The hunt is not usually so eventful."

"Sit, Master Edu." Ziza did not bother to turn her head to address him. "Spill his blood later if you must. But we are in need of all houses to cast a vote."

Edu sighed darkly and sat back down. Yes, he would break Navaa's legs later. But now, Edu needed the cretin not screaming in agony. Very well.

"We are agreed that the girl's expulsion from the ceremony while remaining a mortal is linked to the warlock's early rise?" Ylena asked.

"Yes, but not even *he* can force the hands of our creators." Otoi sniffed dismissively. "The Ancients did this. Not he.

Perhaps they simply wished him awake for someone that may change our world."

"Master Edu has had enough of the debate." Ylena's tone was sharp. Edu's own emotions were leaking into her own. "We shall vote. Who wishes to spare the girl's life?"

Otoi, Ziza, and Navaa each lifted a hand. Three votes to spare her life. That left Edu and Kamira voting against. Maverick was looking thoughtfully down at the table, tapping a finger on the gleaming polished wood surface.

"Master Edu reminds you all that a tie goes in the king's favor," Ylena said.

"We are aware." Navaa rolled his eyes.

Yes, he would be snapping Navaa's legs later.

Maverick sighed heavily, his one visible yellow eye closing as his brow furrowed in thought. It smoothed after a long moment. "I vote to spare her. I cannot condemn her to death on suspicion and paranoia. If proof presents itself that Aon has anything to do with the girl's condition, I change my vote."

Kamira snickered. "As long as she isn't my pet, I suppose I do not care."

Edu growled in frustration once more and resisted the urge to plant his fist through the table's surface.

"It is rare such things do not go in your favor," Ylena silently reminded him. *"Take this with grace."*

The warlock had a hand in this madness. Edu was certain of it. And he would not leave this world in that fetid necromancer's hands, not now, not until the last of their world vanished into the void. Edu would not return to his crypt. Treaty be damned.

"Do not make me speak of such things, my master," Ylena warned. *"You will bring them to unite against you."*

"Then do not say it." Edu leaned back into the rough-hewn chair, and it creaked under his weight as he shifted. He wore no armor in his own home. Instead, it was the collection of

leathers, furs, fabrics, and chains that would mark him a king in the days gone by, when humans were honest and sincere to their nature. When they would worship the dragon and understand that life was to be taken and spent in battle, not toiling in studies and seeking betterment. He missed those days when he would walk the cold lands of the Earthen north as a god.

"Call a tourney," he commanded, keenly understanding how he wished to indulge himself. He wanted to feel the bones snap beneath his feet, and a skull crush between his fingers. He would smell the scent of blood in the air, before venting his darker desires upon some young thing or another. Tomorrow, he would find a new partner—someone fresh to him, someone whose innocence he could destroy. In his wariness, he sought destruction. It was a childish response to the unfolding events, but he did not care. He cared little to curb his appetite.

"Master Edu will call a tourney for tomorrow, his farewell custom. All of you will be expected to attend, as usual."

Ah, Ylena. Always trying to smooth the sharp spikes to his desires. Tonight, he would thank her himself. He smirked beneath his mask and let his mind wander from his troubles, if only for the moment.

* * *

Aon held the shattered, broken frame in his arms. She was tiny and frail. Every movement she took fractured a new bone in her body. Her labored breaths were scratchy and pained. She was in agony.

She would not live long.

It was for the best.

Yet he wept. He wept, for those mismatched, mangled eyes of hers gazed up at him, and he knew they were sightless. But in them was reflected such love; such pure and simple adoration that he knew... it was all that she could feel.

He held her in his arms. She would die within minutes. Her body could not support life; the tragic, malformed creature was not meant to live.

She loved him, after all.

And nothing in this forsaken world was meant to feel such a thing.

Such was the law of nature.

But he would hold her while she died. Hold her while her breaths became more shallow with every passing attempt. While her heartbeat began to still, her thin, deformed lips tried to speak, tried to tell him that she loved him.

She was meant to die.

It was for the best.

And yet, he wept.

Rising from his dreams took time. It took precious moments he did not know if he could spare. The girl was Edu's prisoner, and while he was left sifting through his memories, she may be dead or dying.

The thought gave him a sense of urgency that surprised him. Why did he care for the little blonde poppet that looked at him with such curiosity and fear? Rarely did the mortals ever capture his attention; rarer still did he pay any mind to those who Fell to his world that were not inked in black.

But this creature had Fallen and been tossed aside. Removed of the mark that brought her here, and yet given no others to replace them. She was gloriously entertaining to him by her own benefit; but now that this development had occurred, she was also dangerous.

For nothing like her had ever been seen before. Not in any recorded history of their ancient world.

And he coveted the things he found interesting. Be they books, artworks, or, in this case, a beautiful blonde child.

He hungered for her. That complicated matters deeply, but my, how it made the game far more challenging.

Navaa.

"Yes, my lord?"

He called to his second in command—his regent—from this place of slumber. He did this often while he was slumbering, keeping track of the waking world through his servant.

There was a girl. Tossed aside by the Ancients. Her name is Lydia.

"I know of her. I was there when she was rejected. Edu has her. Our spies say that she is in the cell and has befriended some wench named Evelyn. I think he plans to execute her soon."

Yes. He had the exact same suspicion.

Keep her safe as long as you can. I will wake soon.

"Of course, my king."

Soon, he would be able to show Lydia just who she had been dealing with... in the flesh.

* * *

When Lydia found herself standing on a black, shining surface surrounded by a void, she knew what to expect. "God *damn it.*" She barely had to wait a half second before she felt a hand drift onto her shoulder from behind her, metallic and cold.

Lydia whirled and staggered away from Aon, who loomed behind her like a specter against the darkness.

"You have finally come to fear me, I see." He sounded somehow disappointed.

"You've attacked me. Twice! You're probably gonna do it a third time."

"I suppose technically I have," he said, sounding annoyed at her pointing out the triviality of it. "First, in this state of dreaming, it hardly counts. Second, both times it was only to wake you from your slumber." When she glared at him silently, Aon shrugged and continued. "Yes, yes. Very well. I enjoy tormenting you. That, I will not deny. But that was the secondary motivation, I assure you."

"Is that supposed to make me feel better?" She took another step back from him. Where the hell she intended on going in a world that didn't exist—surrounded by literally nothing—she didn't know, but it wasn't going to stop her from trying to keep as much distance between them as possible.

"No. I suppose it would not. But this is new. This is not terror I see in your face, is it." His voice lowered dangerously. "It is *disgust*. I suppose I should not be surprised, though I am disappointed." He took a step toward her, stalking her like a great black panther. Lydia took another step back. "Has that twit in the other cell told you all about my reputation? Regaled you with tales of those who enter my care and in what state they return? That even amongst a society of monsters and demons, I am reviled?"

Aon lunged at her, and Lydia screamed, falling backward. His hands caught her wrists, and she was suddenly yanked toward him and spun around. Before she could react, he had her pinned against him, her back to his chest. His clawed fingers were once again around her throat, threatening to dig deeper, as they had the last time.

"*Well?*" His anger had come out of nowhere.

"She said y-you—" Lydia could barely get the words out. "That you torture people. Peel their skin off. Bleed them dry. Boil them in water up to their necks and—"

Aon cackled in laughter, and when he spoke again, his voice was filled with cold, quiet cruelty. "That is a new one. And do you believe her?"

"Should I?"

"Edu will kill you quickly." His arm around her tightened. "He will not savor the deed. Do you know that he is the kinder of us? Oh, how his heart used to be so filled with compassion and sympathy. Now, he is nearly as cruel as I am. It is by my hand he has come to be this way."

"Why're you doing this to me?" Lydia tilted her head back away from his gauntlet, even if it forced her to press her head against his shoulder. His long dark hair brushed against her cheek as he towered over her.

"Edu will destroy you because he despises me. Now, not by my actions, but by their words, you find me revolting as well." Aon threw her from him suddenly. The movement sent her to the ground, and she landed hard on the smooth surface. Wide-eyed and terrified, she could only watch as he stepped up to loom over where she was now sitting, propped up on her hands. "All that little wench has told you? It is spoken truth!"

"Aon, I don't understand. If she wasn't lying, then why are you angry?"

Aon snarled and turned away from her, pacing angrily at her feet. Lydia stayed put, fearing what he might do if she stood back up.

Why was he so furious with her? It made no sense. She hadn't done anything, and he had flown off the handle. He said he was insane—so did everyone else—but this didn't look like insanity. Just the idea that Evie had been telling her about him had sent him into a furious rage.

Oh.

A light bulb went off in her head as pieces began to click into place.

There was something to be said for having a sense of self-preservation. Sadly, she wasn't the proud owner of any—she never really had a good concept of when to keep her mouth shut. It was part of the reason she had gone into the profession of working with the dead, after all.

Now he had pushed her, literally and figuratively, too far. Her temper snapped. He was acting like a schoolyard bully, and hell if she was going to die or be tortured and take it with a smile. "You can pick on me all you want. But I'm not the one you're mad at. You hate them all, don't you? Worse, you can't —" Her words were broken off as she shrieked.

Aon darted toward her, knocking her arms out from under her and sending her flat to the ground. He was now kneeling over her, straddling her waist, pinning her down. His clawed gauntlet was around her throat, his other hand supporting his weight by her head as he leaned over her.

"I can't *what*?" His words were a vicious hiss. When all Lydia could do was hopelessly stammer, he tightened his grasp. "No. You began your foolish brigade of words. You will finish it! I can't *what*?"

Yep. This was going to hurt. But she stared him down as she finished her sentence. "You can't stand that they hate you back."

What she didn't expect was his laughter. It was cruel, cold, and biting. It was unkind, and it was a sound she hoped she would never hear again. She had heard him laugh before, but not like this.

Shifting his gloved hand to twist in her hair before leaning his weight on it, he kept her pinned and unable to move as he wandered his claw down her throat. "How very keenly observant. Do you think you understand me now, my dear?"

"No, I—"

"Are at your wits' end, I know. Terrified and tormented. But you chose the wrong man on whom to vent your frustrations." He continued to let his hand meander downward, clearly in no rush. He drifted it over the swell of her breast, down her side, and stopped. He lifted his hand to rest the tip of his pointer finger against her, in between two of her ribs.

"I'm sorry, I—"

"No. You are no such thing. You only wish to avoid what I am now going to do to you in return for your cutting remarks." Slowly, he pressed the tip of his scalpel-sharp metal nail into her. "This time, you shall not wake up until I allow it. You will learn to treat my kindness with more respect."

The pain made her gag. Lydia cried out as she felt the blade pierce her skin. Dreams weren't supposed to be painful! But this was no normal dream, after all. Gritting her teeth, she managed to glare up at him. "This has been you being kind?" If he was going to do this, Lydia would go down swinging. "More like you getting off."

"It takes much more than this, trust me." He hummed. "This? This is child's play." Aon began pressing the digit further into her body, sinking it past the first knuckle, then the second, slipping past the barbed layers of his metal gauntlet like the points of an arrow. The path back out would cause severe damage. "If you have decided to revile me as the others, I will give you due cause of your own without relying on the words of others."

Her mind went white with pain, and she lost track of what was happening for a moment. When she came back around, his finger was sunk into her body to his knuckle. The feeling of cold metal was against her face, and she realized he had pressed his masked forehead against hers. Aon was talking to her—quietly, soothingly. She couldn't grasp his words at first. "—if you cannot withstand this, you cannot weather what they will do to you. And I fear I will let no one else destroy you now, but me, Lydia." His voice was gentle and coaxing. "Come, now, Lydia. You can do this. Show me you can do this."

It hurt. Dear God, it hurt. She let out a single sob and felt the tears run down along her cheeks and into her hair. As she moved, he seemed to realize she had come to and let out a small hmh in his throat and pulled his head slowly away from hers.

"There you are. I thought I had broken you so soon."

"Fuck... you..." It hurt to breathe, so she opted to use the air wisely.

Aon chuckled. "There will be time for that later. I came

here to tell you something, my little darling, before you angered me so perfectly." Aon twisted his finger in her body, and she gagged in pain badly enough she couldn't even scream. "But now you've gone and distracted me, and I cannot for the *life* of me remember what it is. Do give me a moment to remember."

Aon's voice was low, quiet, and would have been sultry if it weren't for his armored finger buried deep in her body. She realized with a sick sense of horror that he was probably enjoying this.

"Ah! I remember now. I will wake within the day. Won't you be so *happy* to see me?"

When he wasn't moving his finger, the pain made her want to throw up, but it was manageable. She had no doubt that if she weren't trapped in a dream where the laws of physics weren't so sacrosanct, she'd have long since gone into shock already.

"Aon." She wasn't even sure what she was trying to say at first. "Let me go home—please."

"No. I fear that is one thing I do not have the power to grant. But, truthfully? Even if I could, I would not." Aon inched himself closer, lowering his head to rest his metal cheek against hers and let his voice whisper quietly into the ear. The smell of old books and leather filled her nose again, mixing with the coppery twinge from the blood pooling and running down her side. "For what glorious fun we will have together."

Her mind went white in pain and then was followed by merciful black as Aon ripped his finger from her body.

FOURTEEN

"Lydia!"

Someone was shouting her name. Lydia was shaking and staring wide-eyed up at the ceiling, her heart pounding in her ears. It was better than where she had just been, trapped in that nothingness with Aon.

Groaning, she put her hands to her face, covering her eyes with her palms. The memory of the feeling of Aon tearing his barbed, gauntleted finger out of her body made her throat feel thick, and her stomach threatened to upend itself. She was overcome by an uncontrollable shiver.

After a pause, Evie nervously piped up. "Was it him again?"

"Yeah."

"How bad was it?"

"The worst part is, I'm sure on his scale, it wasn't anything." Finally, she felt like she could sit up. There was a faint rectangle of light, marked by bars, sitting in the middle of the floor. The glow was turquoise. What the hell could cast light that color? Tracing its source, she saw a small window high up on the wall she hadn't noticed before. It had always been dark outside, every time she had seen a window. But now, there was a moon on the other side of the bars, and it was far too large to be the one she recognized.

Far too large, and far too teal.

More proof she wasn't on Earth. Not that she really needed anything to add to the list. But she wanted to see it anyway. Shifting to the window to catch a better sight of the large, circular, glowing shape. The rest of the sky was pitch black.

It was hauntingly beautiful in its own right, even if it was a keen reminder of how doomed she was. But something seemed to be missing. "Are there stars here?"

"No." Her tone heavily hinted she might miss the sight of them. "But! We have more than our fair share of moons here on Under." It was adorable how she was trying to provide an upside to the conversation considering their situation. "All of them are big and weird colors. Very pretty, though. We don't have a sun, so they give off the light things need to grow."

Walking back over to the edge of the wall of bars between her and Evie, she sank to the ground. Evie scooted over to sit next to her, reaching out to hold her hand.

It was a simple and childish gesture but... screw it. She could use all the comfort she could get. Taking Evie's hand, she squeezed it gently. They fell into a long silence. It let her think over what had happened. On what Aon had done in her dream, everything he'd said. "Aon is a piece of work, huh?"

Evie giggled and stopped at the look Lydia gave her. "Sorry. It's not funny. But you were funny. What'd he do?"

"I pissed him off. I had to open my fat face and mouth off at him. Now, he's going to torture me in person, as soon as he wakes up. That is, if Edu doesn't kill me first."

"I'm so sorry, bunny." Evie shifted closer to the bars and turned to face her, squeezing her hand tighter. "I wish there was something I could do."

Yeah, I'm getting to that.

"Edu wants me dead because he thinks I'm a threat. Aon

wants to pull me apart at the seams for a laugh. Either way, I'm fucking doomed. I need to figure out a way to escape."

"Oof. Really? That's a great way to get killed. What if you ask Edu for help? Tell him what Aon is doing. They're rivals. Maybe Edu can protect you."

Lydia snickered. "Or kill me faster because Aon is after me."

Evie sighed. "Yeah, could be. Edu's a lot of things, but he's not mean. If you need help, if you tell him Aon's gonna hurt'cha, he might step in. Edu's not a bad man. Better than what Aon'll do when he wakes up."

The idea of being at Aon's mercy made her stomach flip in fear, worse than any of the rest of this. He had already shown her exactly how violent he could be. Death at Edu's hands was going to be the faster, easier way out. But what she had said to Aon was the truth; she didn't want to die.

"Maybe. I'm dead anyway. It might be worth a try."

Evie balled up her hand into a fist and lightly nudged Lydia in the shoulder. "That's the spirit!"

A door opened out of her line of sight—the entrance into the dungeon or cell block, whatever they wanted to call it. A pair of footsteps approached. The same guard who had brought her food was back, and trailing behind him was Tim. Leather coat, zippers, white shirt, and all. She wondered if he realized he was a walking cliché, but then again, if he was the only "greaser" here, maybe it wound up on the other side and was back to being original.

The guard had a circle of keys and was fishing for the right one to unlock her cell door.

"Hey, toots. Time to go." Tim shoved a thumb toward the door out of the space.

Lydia stood, fear flooding back to her like an old friend. "What? Time to go where?"

"Oh, simmer. Edu's throwing a contest, and there's a party at the end of it, and he's ordered you to be there." Tim shrugged, shoving his hands into the pockets of his leather coat casually. "Told me to bring you. So here I am, bringing you."

Contest. Lydia hoped it was volleyball. Maybe table tennis. Something told her it was not going to be either. Hopefully, she wasn't going to wind up being the piñata at the celebration.

"Fine." She threw her hands up in frustration. "Whatever."

"Try to enjoy the party!" Evie waved goodbye. "It'll be a ball!"

She rolled her eyes. "How am I supposed to enjoy the party? I'm probably going to die right after it."

"All the more reason to have fun." Her smile didn't waver.

Before Lydia could really muster a flabbergasted response, she was ushered out of the cell and down the stone hallway with Tim at her side.

Edu's keep looked like a medieval castle—if it were built in Norway. As they walked through the hallways silently, she could only take in the sights. Shields and weapons were hanging on the walls in droves, wooden, roughly carved monsters and animals hanging from beams and joists in decoration. Celtic knots and strange, winding designs were carved into every surface. She felt like she was in a building that had no business existing in this day and age.

The kitchen in the cathedral had been a hodge-podge of devices from all eras. Lydia wondered if their world followed the same rule. Every place here was a slice taken out of time. A Gothic cathedral and now a Nordic Viking castle. Weird.

"Remember what I told you about culture in Under?" Tim scratched his stubble. "'Bout how we like, eh... pretty much everything?"

Lydia put her hand over her eyes with a groan. The feast would be a pile of food and a pile of bodies. It wasn't that she was shy, or that she wasn't fully aware of all the things that people could do together. She fully supported people enjoying themselves, and she wasn't a prude herself, by any means. She was no stranger to sex or having fun, even if she wasn't prone to fits of excess.

She just didn't want to goddamn deal with it right now.

"Great. Just great, Tim. Can I go back to my cell now?"

Laughing, Tim pushed through a large door. "You're fun, toots."

Suddenly, she felt fresh air on her face—outside air—for the first time since coming to Under.

It felt amazing, a real breeze of fresh air. Lydia hadn't realized how claustrophobic she had been feeling until right then. Tim was trying to drag her forward, but she yanked her arm out of his grasp and took a step to the side, needing some distance from him. For a moment, for a brief instant of time, she stared agog at the world in front of her. She had only been indoors until now. For the first time, she saw this world of Under.

What she saw was beautiful.

Full of the sharp contrast between light and dark, it took her a moment to realize she was looking at a courtyard, sharply lit by the turquoise moon above. It cast stark shadows of each cobblestone of a large courtyard in front of her.

She was standing on a series of steps leading up to the door. On the other side of the courtyard was a row of trees that looked like an ancient forest, trees with old and twisting limbs that wound around each other, too dark to see much in the dim lighting. Above her was the moon in all its blue-green glory— and sure enough, there were no stars around it, nothing to hint of a universe beyond this world.

"C'mon." Tim was a few steps down from the landing and gestured for her to follow him. "I know. I know this is a lot. But please. We can't be late."

Snapping back into the moment, she realized there was indeed a carriage in the courtyard. At the head of the wagon were two—well, she assumed they were supposed to be horses if you had crossbred one with a cricket. They held the body shape of a horse but had an exoskeleton instead of fur. Jagged, sharp plates of what almost looked like armor layered on top of each other in hinges and trailed backward. Two large horns rose from their heads, jagged and curling in long spirals behind them.

Their eyes were those of an insect, though, faceted and strange. One clonked its hoof into the ground and tossed its head, cracking its horns against its back in impatience. Their back legs bent the wrong way entirely and were far too large, just like a bug's.

Lydia hadn't realized she had taken a step back until Tim's hand was on her wrist, holding her in place. "You're okay, doll. They're harmless, just like horses."

They weren't any weirder than that graspling she had met, Lydia tried to remind herself. But still, she couldn't relax her shoulders—or anything else—as she walked down the stairs with Tim toward the carriage. Okay. Bug-horses. Weird, horned, evil, armored bug-horses. That used to be people. That probably ate people, because everything in Under was a carnivore. No problem. She kept talking to herself in her mind, trying to convince herself she was not about to die.

It wasn't really working.

* * *

To Edu, there was no greater release than feeling the life exit the body of a fallen opponent.

He dug his sword deep through the chest cavity of his foe, pinning the corpse of his opponent to the ground. Driving his blade deep into the dirt, he twisted it, feeling the resistance of the packed surface beneath the flesh more than the bone itself.

The woman who lay at his feet was one of his own house. A fierce creature who had sought to face him in battle for many years now. He was immensely proud of her for her valiant show.

Yanking his sword from her ribcage sent a spray of crimson

blood across the packed dirt of the Colosseum floor. The crowd hollered and cheered, applauding the violence more than his victory. He was undefeated in battle, after all. None were expected to win against him.

What was to be celebrated was how long and how well a challenger might stand against him.

He saluted his adversary, pounding his gauntleted fist to his chest. The crowd cheered, celebrating the pageantry. The freedom. The gore.

Rumor would already have flown of Aon's imminent return. Yet none knew—save himself and Ylena, who was privy to his thoughts—that he intended not to return to his own crypt in exchange, as was custom.

It could spark a war, his contempt of the agreement between him and the warlock. But he could not return to his crypt just yet. He could not leave it to that bastard to bend the development with the human woman to his whim and use it for his own personal gain.

Turning from his dead opponent, he stalked from the stage of the Colosseum without any further ado. He had a need for his armor to be removed and scrubbed of the blood that now dripped from his breastplate in small dabs as he walked. There was another chance this evening for him to drown his troubles, if not in alcohol, as his compatriots would, then in flesh.

"You must not trouble so," Ylena said to him as he walked into the antechamber outside the main floor of the battleground. His squires were already attending to him, unclipping the massive hunks of armor from his shoulders and undoing the series of straps and buckles it took to secure it all together.

"And how am I not? Aon wakes within the week. He will usurp my throne—"

"Such as was agreed, my lord."

"He will usurp my throne." Never would he truly accept this

treaty of his with Aon. He knew the warlock felt the same. *"And whatever secret behind the girl he will use to his own ends!"*

"Such is his right."

"I should kill her before he has a chance." He clenched his fists. They were free of the metal gauntlet he had worn a moment earlier, and he was happy to feel his own nails press into his palm.

"The council agreed."

"Damn the council."

"Be wary, my lord. Our world has been left unchanged and predictable in all ways since The Great War. Our world is dying, my king. She is the first anomaly we have seen since those days. I would not snuff her out of spite alone."

"Spite?" Edu lowered his head, trying to keep his rage at bay. *"I seek to save this world from what Aon may do!"*

"She may be the key to our survival. You may yet see Under destroyed in keeping her from Aon." Ylena's words were the truth. While she did not view the future as Ziza might, Ylena saw Edu's mind as clearly as one might look through a pane of glass.

Their world was dying. With every day that passed, it was found shrinking and fading slowly to black, disappearing into the void. Even as their world aligned with the world of Earth, and they took souls as they were granted, nothing changed. Nothing was unexpected. Not until the mortal girl arrived. Not until Lydia was cast into the blood and was refused.

It was this potential that Edu would not let fall into Aon's hands. Not while Edu slept, ignorant and absolved in his crypt. Edu would speak to the girl. Learn of her dealings with the warlock. Tomorrow, the council would vote on what to do with the girl. Tomorrow, she would die.

He did not enjoy the thought of needless permanent death. Even if it was a mortal such as her. She had shown such potential—such spirit. It saddened Edu that Lydia would not come to join the fabric of their world.

Tonight, he would meet with the girl. He would have from her all she knew of her condition. And if not that, then perhaps he could find another way to fill her evening.

* * *

Thank God for booze.

Lydia was at a long beer hall style table with benches and tables set into rows. The place was enormous, with vaulted ceilings in thatched straw spanning between whole debarked trees that were used to support the giant structure. Hundreds of people were grouped around tables, laughing and chatting. They all had symbols, and masks of six different colors like Tim had told her. Music was being played by several people at once in various places. Someone had a lute, someone had a guitar, and a group of people were singing a shanty over by one section of the room.

The tournament had been in a massive, Roman Colosseum style stadium, where contenders had fought to the death in matches. Every time someone was about to die, she had to bury her head in her hands. Tim had laughed at her and found her chagrin incredibly amusing.

Speaking of, it seemed like Tim was back for a second helping of her discomfort. "Better slow down, doll." He sat on the bench next to her.

"Fuck off, Tim." She glared down into her glass of wine. "I'd like to go back to my dinky jail cell now."

"Aren't you having fun?"

"Seriously?" She shot him a look with an arched eyebrow.

Tim laughed again, louder this time. "You're all right, kid. Sorry, I didn't come here to chat. Edu wants to see you."

Lydia groaned and lowered her head. This wasn't going to go well. No matter what.

Tim got up and gestured for her to follow him again. With a long breath, she pushed herself up from the table. She nearly caught her dress on the corner of the bench she was sitting on. She wasn't used to wearing things with skirts, and the long, gray, lace-up number she had been given to wear was a far cry from anything she'd typically ever pick out of a rack.

In the shadows of the room, she could see figures hunched in the darkness, enjoying themselves. Many of them in groups. Well, Tim hadn't been kidding. She tried to think about a world where nobody could die, nobody could get pregnant or sick.

Where society didn't lecture them about how that kind of thing was immoral and wrong.

Without all of that, and with an eternity of life stretching out in front of them, she could see why pleasure of any kind would become important. When your world didn't change, and you couldn't die or raise a family, what else was there? Boredom?

Of course, everyone was drunk. Of course, everyone loved violence and sex. It didn't matter. There was none of the fallout to worry over. Tim and Lydia had to step around a couple who were blocking the path. The man had the woman's legs around his waist, and she was pinned to the wood beam of the hall by his impatient, passionate thrusts.

She couldn't help but feel her face go warm in a blush. She wasn't a prude, but she'd never just walked past two people casually screwing. Her college experience hadn't been like that —med school and all. People were too busy studying. Or maybe she went to the wrong parties.

Tim brought her through a door at the end of the room that went to a smaller chamber. She took one step through it, saw what was in front of her, and immediately turned around and faced the wall.

Holy shit.

Part of her wanted to laugh at how ridiculous it was. The other part of her wanted to stick a fork into her leg.

It took Lydia a long time to work up the nerve to turn back around to face forward. Tim was cracking up, laughing hysterically next to her. He was doubled over, his hands on his thighs, as he fought to breathe through his laughing.

To his credit, Tim had tried to warn her. Sex was not taboo here. Therefore, it was on full display. She did her best to ignore the writhing bodies that hung around the edges of the room on piles of pillows or up against the walls. It had been what was in the center of the room that had made her "nope out."

Edu was lying there on a large circular platform that was covered in pillows. It had a headboard, and he was propped up against it. The man was completely naked except for his mask, and it was the first time she had seen him without his armor.

The mask was the only reason she knew it was him, with its deep crimson, dragon-like skull. He didn't have a helmet on, so his horns were gone, but the face was the same. He had the appearance of a bodybuilder or a professional wrestler. His entire body was covered in red ink markings and scars.

Two women were... well, enjoying him. Their nude bodies were writhing over his in complete abandon. Lydia looked at the ceiling, quickly decided that looking up was the only safe bet. Her face felt on fire. Tim was still snickering desperately from her side, enjoying her embarrassment.

"Shut up, Tim," she muttered.

That only made him laugh harder. "I mean, if Edu's too intimidating to start with, I'm nothing to sneeze at, but I'd be glad to warm you up for him."

She was sure his proposition was just as sincere as it was meant to goad her. That, she could react to. She turned to look at Tim, balled up her fist, and punched him hard in the arm. He let out a yelp and grabbed the afflicted spot. It was more out of surprise than pain, she was sure. His startled expression bloomed into a grin as if he was glad she fought back. "Oh, you're a fighter, huh? I can get on board with that. C'mere, baby. Give us a kiss."

"Fuck off, Tim, or I swear to God I'll—"

"Lord Edu requests you bring her forward."

Lydia knew that voice. She turned her head and desperately tried to avoid looking at the two women who were fawning over Edu's prone body. Standing by the side of the platform was a woman in a long, red dress with straight black hair and a mask that covered the upper half of her face. She had been there on the streets of Boston when Edu had first chased her and Nick.

Stepping forward, she tried very, very hard not to watch the two nude women as they were lavishing Edu's massive body— all of it—with hungry mouths. This was a really awkward way to have a conversation.

"These two were taken in the Ceremony of the Fall yesterday, with your friend Nicholas," the woman in red said. Something told Lydia the woman's words weren't totally her own. Add it to the list of weird shit she had seen in the past few days. "They have accepted their place. They have come to embrace their king with joy."

"Good for them." Snark was going to get her killed, but it was all she had left right now, especially with the pompous explanation of the display going on in front of her that she'd just been given.

"He invites you to join them."

"Is Nick okay?" Lydia ignored his offer entirely and fought the urge to run for the door.

Edu snorted once, seemingly annoyed that she preferred to worry over her friend than to climb onto the bed.

"Your friend has Fallen to the House of Moons, with the

shifters. He is more than 'okay.'" The woman in red paused and seemed to listen to something. "Master Edu desires your company this evening. Will you oblige him?"

"No. I'm not going to have sex with him to save my life."

"It has nothing to do with saving your life. He thought perhaps you would merely like to enjoy your evening as his guest."

Putting her hands over her face, she laughed. She was mentally exhausted by everything and everyone she had met. "No, thank you. I'm flattered, but no."

"Would you rather lay with the warlock?"

Lydia couldn't help but look up at Edu in wide-eyed shock. When the man let out a long sigh and pushed the women gently off him, she knew she had played right into his hand. *Fuck, fuck, fuck!*

Edu climbed off the bed to stand in front of her. Even without his armor, he was huge. He must have been seven feet tall or more and broad as a truck. The man was all stacked muscle. His arms and his chest were marked with scars mingled with rows of the esoteric red writing. Edu had the body of a man who used it for a purpose, not just for show. He had long, curly, auburn brown hair. It fell along the sides of his crimson mask in waves.

Lydia didn't dare look down. She'd seen enough to know he was to scale. She didn't need more proof.

"It is no use lying. How do you know of Aon?" the woman in red asked.

"He..." Oh God. *Well, here goes nothing.* Or everything. "He's—he's been showing up in my dreams. Threatens me, taunts me. This last time, I—he tortured me." She went cold at the memory of Aon's claw buried into her ribs. Lydia pressed a hand to her side reflexively as she shuddered.

"Why?" the woman asked. For Edu, she was beginning to suspect. Edu had yet to say a word.

"I was stupid and opened my fat mouth and said something I shouldn't have." She stared directly ahead into Edu's massive chest. The markings on his chest were winding and cryptic. They matched the marks she had seen on people's faces or arms. But Edu had a great deal more than anyone else Lydia had seen so far. He was a king, and marks equaled power, she remembered. "I might have told him to get over himself? Kinda?"

Edu chuckled. It was a low, deep sound, and not unpleasant.

Lydia jumped, startled, as he put a hand on her shoulder, his large palm resting suddenly against where it joined her neck. His touch was hot, and he curled his fingers around behind her. His thumb rested against her jawline, and she felt the pad run along her in a slow line. It was rough, raspy—calloused, but not harsh.

She turned her head away, worried he was going to hit her. But, raising his other hand to rest against her jaw on the other side, he tilted her head to look up to him.

"You say you have no dealings with the warlock? That it is not a willing arrangement between you two?"

"Have you met him? *Fuck* no." That brought a louder laugh out of Edu, dashing any of her concerns about speaking out of turn. "He shows up in my dreams, chases me around, taunts me with that damn claw of his. I just... I just want to go home. Please. Can you help me?"

"Master Edu apologizes that he cannot grant such a wish." The lady in red spoke again.

Lydia winced and shut her eyes.

One of Edu's large hands lifted from her face to stroke her hair. "He asks again if you will join him this evening. Master Edu respects and appreciates the strength that burns within you. Your time here in Under has been nothing but suffering. He wishes to impart some joy and pleasure into it."

"I'm sure it's a great honor to sleep with a king, but—"

"He has no intention of sleeping," the woman in red interjected.

She slapped a hand over her eyes. "Right, well, okay, to screw a king, then. But... I'd rather not, sorry."

Edu sighed and turned her head to look up at him, a large hand cupped under her jaw. Even as the woman in red spoke, she knew the words came from the behemoth in front of her. "It grieves him then, that you will not accept his comfort before he must take your life come the morning."

"*What?* Why?" She jumped back away from him, not caring if it ticked him off now.

"The council voted to save your life on the condition that the warlock had nothing to do with you. If he resides inside your dreams, if he has pledged to claim you, your danger to this world is confirmed. You must die before the warlock rises."

"No." Lydia took another step back. "Please, no. I don't have anything to do with this!"

"Master Edu knows this. He knows it is by no work of your own that you have been dealt this hand. But the deed must be done, regardless. That is why he wished to spend the night with you."

"When were you going to tell me? Before or after you screwed me?" She barely noticed the scene she was creating had interrupted the activities of everyone else. They all stopped to watch.

"Never." Edu shrugged as the woman talked. "He would have snapped your neck while you slept. He does not desire you to suffer or be afraid. Your plight is unfortunate enough."

For the second time in two days, she was going to tell off a king. Well, if she was going to die in the morning, at least she would go out with a bang. "Go rot in hell, you overgrown sack of shit. I'm out. I'm done. You can go back to your little fuck-stage, you freak."

And with that, she stormed out of the room. Tim went to

stop her, but she shoved him out of the way, knocking him into a post with the unexpected outburst. She did her best to keep her pace regular, even if she wanted to run for the far door of Edu's hall and never stop.

"Hey! Doll!" Tim called after her.

She headed for the door, trying to stay to the sides and the shadows as best she could. She needed space to think. She had to try to escape Edu's imprisonment. She had to flee Under. Somehow. Scrambling, she attempted to come up with a plan. Passing a table, she noticed a fork and a knife lying on the wood surface. Without thinking, she picked them up and sat on a bench to slip them into one of the knee-high boots they had given her to wear for the evening.

There wasn't the slightest idea in her head of what she was going to do to escape a world like this with a knife and fork, but... hey. It was better than nothing.

Tim was on her quickly and stood in front of her. She looked up at him and wiped at the tears that ran down her face.

"Toots, that... that was dumb. I get it. I really get it. But that was dumb."

"What would you have done?"

"The same thing." Tim huffed a half. "Edu told me to bring you back to your cell. Said to tell you that your execution will come in the morning."

"Great. Yeah, I know, the king's busy. He has some people to screw." All the way back to the carriage, and through the trip back to Edu's keep, she was silent.

In the morning, she was going to die. There was no stopping Edu. Even if the man was just an ordinary mortal, he outweighed her and outclassed her several times over. She couldn't stop him if he wanted to snap her neck, let alone whatever else a supernatural king of Under could muster up to end her life.

Right now, she had a fleeting, dim hope. She didn't have a

plan yet. She didn't know how she was going to pull it off. But she had to try to run. She had to try to escape. It was that or accept death. Something she could never do.

She'd fail.

But damn it all, she had to try.

FIFTEEN

It hadn't taken Evie long to press for details when Lydia returned to the jail cell. After she told her new friend that she'd opted not to sleep with Edu, Evie was clearly disappointed. In fact, she seemed to skip right over the impending death sentence part entirely.   ‹

"Are you serious? You could've slept with him?" Evie pouted.

"He's going to kill me!"

"You didn't know that at the time." She let out a *hrumph.*

"You're missing the point, Evie."

"I would've done it anyway. At least you'd have had something nice to go out on." Evie was lying on the floor of her cell by the bars, her ankle across a bent knee and hands behind her head like this was just a girl's night and a sleepover. Not a dire situation where Lydia was going to be executed tomorrow. "Have you seen the package on that man? Romping with him? Let me tell you, it's just..." Evie whistled, then put her fingers to her lips and kissed them like a French chef.

That got an overwhelmed laugh out of Lydia. She stopped

her pacing to look at the girl incredulously. "You've slept with him?"

"Of course. Pretty much everyone has."

"That's disgusting and doesn't make it any better."

"Things're different here." Evie waved her hand dismissively. "Nobody turns away a straight six like that man. Nobody would've judged you for it. Nobody here hasn't already slept with Edu—man or woman."

"Just... no." Making a face, she shook her head.

"Was it the crowd scenario? Are you shy? You're not a virgin, are you?"

"Hell, no." She felt indignant at the idea that she might be. "Evie! I'm going to be executed in the morning. Focus."

"Sorry." Evie giggled.

Sighing, she hung her head and looked down at the fork and knife in her hand. She was standing against a world filled with monsters with nothing more than *dinnerware*. It was so stupid.

Even if Edu wasn't going to kill her, Aon was worse. The memory of his touch on the back of her neck, the cold metal of his mask against her face, the smell of old books and leather, the feeling of his claw buried in her body—all made her shiver.

"Bunny?" Evie sat up.

"I have to get out of here. Out of Under." Turning the cutlery over in her hand, she wondered what the hell she was going to do with it. "If this place and Earth are still aligned, can I get home?"

"Well, technically, there's a gate. But it isn't—"

"What gate? Where?" Eagerly, she went to the bars that separated them. Those was the first words of hope she'd heard all night.

"Uh... well, in Yej, in the city square, there's a portal for general use. But it's miles away," Evie's yellowish eyes were wide.

"Please don't tell me you'd try to make it there. You wouldn't make it through the woods."

"I'm dead anyway. I'm dead no matter what I do. Even if Edu changes his mind, have you ever met Aon?"

"No..." Evie admitted. "He was king when I was taken, but he doesn't socialize. I never saw him. He's a recluse."

"I have." She felt the claws on her skin, saw that single gaping black hole of an eye socket watching her. It felt like he was standing right behind her, and she resisted the urge to glance over her shoulder. It gave her the heebie-jeebies. "Even if Edu changed his mind and let me live, Aon will come for me and tear me to pieces. If the monsters in the woods get me, I don't care. I'm dead anyway. At least if something in the woods gets me, I'll have died trying."

Evie sighed heavily. "Okay, bunny." With that, she leaned her head against the bars and reached out her hand, palm up. Lydia had no idea why for a moment until she realized the girl was asking for the cutlery.

Trusting the girl not to just merely chuck the knife and fork across the room, she handed the two pieces of silverware to her. Evie closed her hand around them and stood, walking toward her cell door. "Pa would've killed me if he knew Stevie taught me how to do this. See, Stevie was this gorgeous little drugstore cowboy. But I didn't care. We were pals, y'know?"

No, Lydia didn't, but she pretended anyway.

Evie was fishing the knife into the lock of her cell from the outside and using the back of the fork to twist. The redhead from Montana was picking the lock of her cell. Usually, Lydia assumed it would require much smaller equipment, but these were medieval style locks meant to be turned with a large and rudimentary key. She fiddled around for a minute before it clicked.

Evie pushed it out an inch, and then looked over at Lydia warily. "You sure 'bout this?"

Not in the slightest. But Lydia had to try. "Just let me out, then lock yourself back in."

"Oh, hell no." Her friend laughed. "We girls gotta stick together. You do this, I do this. Besides, Edu's gonna kill us both." The girl's smile never faded. "Might as well go together."

Evie pushed the door of her cell open and walked around to Lydia's and began picking the lock, her tongue sticking slightly out of her mouth, pinched between her teeth. The silly expression didn't do anything to mar how pretty the girl was. Big eyes, freckles, moppish red hair that was wild around her head. No wonder Edu had already slept with her.

When it clicked, she let out a triumphant "ta-dah!" and stuck her arms out over her head, cutlery still in hand.

Stepping out of her cell, she hugged the other woman.

Evie giggled and hugged her back, smiling broadly. "Cash or check?" It took Lydia a long and confused moment to realize that she was asking if Lydia planned on kissing her. She poked Lydia on the nose. "I recommend check, as we're about to become serious criminals."

"Let's get out of here." She chuckled and let Evie go.

Her friend handed her the fork, opting to keep the knife for herself.

Great. Now she didn't even have a knife. *Fear me and my fork, ageless monsters of Under!* It made her snort in laughter. "God, this is ridiculous."

"You said it." Evie was already creeping toward the door, pressed up against the stone wall dramatically, even though nobody was there to see them. She waved Lydia on, urging her to follow.

And so, she did.

* * *

Edu was lying sprawled out on his bed, a thick fur blanket pulled halfway up over him. He had returned to his home before ending the night by taking one of the new Fallen to his chambers for the rest of the evening.

It was the young girl with the large black eyes and dark hair that Lydia had protected in a pathetic if noble attempt during the first Fall. The next night, she had gone into the pond a weeping, screaming, and terrified child, and had risen a fiery wonder. The Ancients had removed the fear that had consumed her.

Kaori was her name, Edu believed. She was a fiendish, wild creature. It made for an entertaining evening. Edu was glad the girl had Fallen to his own house, the crimson mark on her forehead unhidden behind a mask.

The girl at his side stirred and shifted her head into his arm. She was so very tiny compared to him. Edu had been concerned he might break her. Yet she had performed admirably. It had been her first time with a man, and he would have predicted tears. What he received instead was a small hellcat who pitched herself headlong into the evening with abandon. She had spoken of a release and freedom, feeling like herself for the first time.

She had almost tired him out.

Almost.

All he had to do was sit back, and merely let the girl explore what it was like to feel alive for the first time. He would have gladly taken Lydia's other friend as well, the boy who had been at her side both times he had gone in search for them. While he had his preferences, he enjoyed the presence of both genders. All were welcome.

Though, he would admit that he had sought them out in anger at being refused. Lydia had turned him down and rejected his offer. Walked away from him as if he were undesirable.

While he had many faults—he was childish, violent, impatient, hedonistic, impulsive—he was never undesirable.

So, he had wished to fill his evening with her old companions. But the boy had Fallen to the House of Moons and was out of his reach. While Kamira could not very well refuse Edu's request to have the boy in his bedchambers, he was undergoing a violent and unpredictable change. He would be wildly out of control of his powers and was likely under the close watch of several of Kamira's higher-ranked and older shapeshifters while they trained him how to keep command over his physical form once more.

Shifters always made for entertaining and challenging bedfellows, but that would be for another night. Besides, all had panned out well in the end. The girl at his side had made up for what the boy might have added to the festivities.

Thoughts drifted once more on Lydia and her fate, where they dwelled. It was a loss to end her life. She was intelligent, fiery, and quick to learn. The way she struck Tim for his goading comments had made Edu grin. Most would have devolved to sobbing for mercy. She faced the doom before her with her head raised. He would have been proud to have her join his house in the Fall. But the Ancients had seen fit to do otherwise. They had seen fit to doom her to death at his hands.

Whatever Aon had said or done in her dreams had left a profound impact upon her. When the topic came up—when she spoke the warlock's name—her face had paled, and her eyes had gone wide. Any doubt that she had been speaking the truth was gone in that moment.

It made it simpler on all fronts once he killed the girl in the morning. Then he could return to his crypt free of concern for what Aon might do with whatever secret she might hide. Perhaps he was dooming his world to its slow decay by taking her life. It was a shame, but he resolved himself to the fact it must be done.

Letting his eyes drift shut behind his mask, he settled himself into the pillows beneath them. Sleep was just about to claim him when he heard the keep's great bell begin to ring.

* * *

Man, it would have been helpful if either of them knew where the hell they were going.

Honestly, she hadn't really been paying attention to the layout when she'd gone through the building with Tim. Stark shadows lined the wood floors, cast by burning torches and the strangely colored moonlight from the windows outside. Evie was from a different house and had no better idea of the layout of the keep than she did.

She spent a moment worrying over Nick. He was in the House of Moons with the shifters, whatever that meant. Her heart broke, worrying about him.

But she couldn't help him—or find out what happened to him—if she was dead in the morning like Edu was planning.

Twenty minutes into their caper, creeping along hallways and ducking into doors, they both went rigid when a bell began to ring. It was the same bell they had heard before, high up in a tower somewhere. They ducked into a doorframe and were huddled close together in the shadows.

"Another ceremony?" Lydia whispered to Evie.

"Dunno. Don't think so," she whispered back.

The sound of rushing footsteps gave them their answer. Lydia leaned her head up against the wall behind her and felt dread creeping over her again.

The jig was up.

Both girls let out quiet groans.

Evie was the first to recover. "C'mon!" Pushing open the door they were leaning against, she stuck her head through, peeking to make sure the room was empty, before walking inside and waving her along. Lydia followed and shut the door behind them as quietly as she could.

In their attempt to dodge guards and get to the exit, they had wound up going up a flight of stairs. The room they were in now looked like somewhere you'd entertain guests. Chairs were lavishly decorated and arranged around a table with an elaborately carved surface, but it was too dark, and too dusty, to see what it was.

Swaths of fabric draped from the wood walls reaching up to the ceilings, ending in colorful fabric pennants and flags painted with sigils and names that were meaningless to her. Ini, Vjo, Rxa, Dtu—the last two she recognized. Edu, Aon. Each flag had a color, Edu in red, Aon in black. The other four must be the colors of the other houses. Blue, purple, white, and green, respectively.

One spot appeared to be missing a flag, ripped loose from its post, only bits of faded, tattered fabric remaining.

The room looked abandoned and unused, like no one had been in here in a very, very long time. Cobwebs were thick in all areas where a spider may have wanted to make a home. Dust was layered like a gray veneer on everything else.

"What is this place?" Lydia furrowed her brow.

"No idea." Evie ran her finger across the table's face curiously. It left a clear line in the absence of the dust on the lacquered surface. She rubbed her hands together to wipe off the detritus and looked back at Lydia with a shrug.

Either way, it was time to get out of here. They froze as they heard footsteps run down the hallway outside the room they had ducked inside. "You! Take the west wing. Take the servants in the kitchens with you. They are not to be harmed, but if they escape, *you* will pay for it."

"Yes, sir!" came a more distant response.

Whoever had hollered was right outside the door. Reflexively, the girls shrank against a window, ducking into a corner, somewhere they might be able to hide behind swaths of ancient curtains should someone burst in on them.

"What do we do?" Evie whispered, clutching to Lydia.

Wrapping her arm around her new friend, she hugged the other woman close. She tried to calm down and quiet the pounding of her heart so she could think.

Where could they go? The hallway was out. There were no other doors. Ceiling and floor were out of the question. That left...

She looked toward the window and saw down out of the building. They were on the second story, but there, just barely lit in the dim turquoise light of a setting moon—was a chance.

A series of flags were hung from a long rope that ran from somewhere above the window down to a nearby building. It was low, squat, and looked like a service building more than part of the rest of the stone keep.

Leaning her head closer to the window, she saw the ropes attached just over the frame on the outside and ran down to the ground, each waving red flags, marked with symbols of a dragon or what-have-you. Edu was a king and decorated his house accordingly, after all.

The angle was a little steep, but it'd work. Correction... it *might* work.

"Hey, Evie..."

"Yeah?"

"Ever hear of a zip line?"

* * *

"Are you sure about this?"

"Yeah?" Lydia shrugged. "It's totally safe. I mean, okay, no, but hey..." She had taken a chair from one of the tables and put it up on the two-foot-thick stone windowsill. Opening the window had been a task, and luckily it hinged on the sides, split

up the middle and swung outward leaving their path unob-
structed. The chair had been necessary to reach the rope that
was secured to a hook over the window. "Details."

Evie was standing beside her, looking up at the arrangement
nervously. "I don't like this."

"I don't really have any other ideas. Do you?" Lifting the
candelabra she had yoinked from one of the tables, she
inspected it for any obvious cracks or anything like that. It was a
heavy forged iron piece, crudely hammered into curls and a
vague attempt at adding detail. It was what she was going to
throw over the rope and grab on the other side. Evie held one in
her own hands, clutching it to herself like it was a shield.

"No." Evie looked down through the window. It was about
a hundred-foot run to the other building the rope was attached
to, and the angle was steep. That and the flags tied every ten feet
weren't going to make it a gentle ride. "But I'm scared."

"Yeah, me too." Climbing up onto the sill, she took a deep
breath. "I'll go first."

"Good. I wasn't going to offer." Evie snickered.

Their time was up. One of the doors to the room clicked
and began to open.

Evie squeaked. "Go!"

"Wh—"

"I'll stall them. Go!" Evie ran toward the other door.

"No, I'm not—" She wouldn't leave the girl behind.

"Otherwise, neither of us will make it," Evie hissed in a loud
whisper. "Don't be a nit. You have a home to go back to. I
don't." Evie threw the second door open and stormed into the
hallway, iron candelabra still in hand. "You'll never take me
alive, coppers!"

With that, Evie took off running and laughing. Lydia heard
the footsteps quickly pursue the girl.

Struggling to calm down, she took a few deep breaths. She
couldn't help Evie now. There wasn't anything she could do

but worry about herself. Turning her attention back to the rope and her insane scheme, she let out a groan. She wasn't sure about this at all. But now, if she didn't at least try, Evie's sacrifice would be for nothing.

Putting the candelabra over the rope, she grabbed it with her other hand. It wasn't that Lydia had a fear of heights, but this was different. Well, shit.

Maybe her hands would slip, or she didn't have enough grip strength to hold on. If she fell and broke her neck, at least everyone's problems would be over. Maybe she'd just shatter both her legs. Y'know, no big deal.

The sound of shouting from the hallway spurred her on. She jumped.

The speed of her descent and the fact that she was slapped in the face with a flag every ten feet made for a hell of a ride. Lydia prioritized two things—don't let go, and don't scream. She tried to just hold on for dear life, squeezing the iron so hard she knew her knuckles must be white.

It wasn't until she saw the side of the small service building at the end of the rope coming at her full tilt that she had the wherewithal to react. She was going to smash into it head-on if she didn't do something.

So, she did something.

Namely, she finally let go. She was only a few feet off the ground now, and she hit the dirt with so much momentum it sent her tumbling over herself, rolling to a stop as a complete mess of limbs.

Grunting in pain, pushed herself up onto her elbows and managed to figure out what end was up, at least. Some dirt had wound up in her mouth, gritty and earthen, and she let out a "pleh" as she tried to clear it. The bruises she was going to have were the least of her concerns right now.

Voices nearby sent her scrambling to her feet, forgetting the pain in her limbs from the impact. Whatever this building was, low and squat and made of rough slabs of wood with a thatched ceiling, she didn't care. She grabbed the nearest door she could see and threw it open, ducking inside.

She shut the door behind her, doing her best not to slam it or make a noise in her fear, and heard the voices pass in front of it. Whatever they were talking about, she couldn't understand the language they were using. French, maybe?

Lydia leaned her back against the door and tried to catch her breath. Oh, poor Evie. *I'm so sorry.*

She could barely see in the darkness of the room. It took a long moment for her eyes to adjust. Was she in a barn? No—a stable. Rows and rows of bays stretched out on either side of her, blocked off with high wood sides. The whole place looked like it had been hacked together by people whose tools were a hand saw and a mallet. It looked like something out of a history documentary, impossibly old, even if it was well kept.

The air was thick with the smell of a animals. Hay, wood, and the reek that came along with beasts being nearby, doing what they did best. There was another smell she recognized from her line of work—the acrid scent of blood.

She could see those bug-horse things in several of the stables, horns arching behind their heads, insectoid eyes and weird exoskeleton bodies. The troughs in front of them were stained crimson with gore and bits of bone. Lydia shuddered, remembering that everything in Under was carnivorous.

Focus! Now was not the time to dwell on meat-eating cricket-horse-monsters. If she didn't get out of here fast, they were going to be the least of her concerns.

Think, Lydia. Think!

She had to come up with a plan. Had to come with some means of escaping. What did she have? What could she use? She had a candlestick, a fork stuffed into her boot, and...

Oh, she was an idiot.

Bug-horses. She had *bug-horses.*

* * *

For a while, it was a mystery where the spitfire of a mortal had gone, until there was shouting from outside. The sound of hooves on packed dirt was enough to send Edu charging through his halls and bursting outside. The stables had been emptied, sending the small herd of horses charging into the darkness, letting out screeches and cries of joy as they broke for freedom in all directions.

Watching the herd flee, he knew one of them would have the girl on its back. It would take time to chase them all down. And now, they had no horses on which to do so. They'd have to wake the wyverns that slept in the rookery to give pursuit. And by then, the girl would have made it to the woods.

His jaw twitched in fury. He stepped down the stairs of his home, and with a gesture of his hand, a crimson pool of fire appeared in front of him. From it rose his own steed, climbing out of the ground as if summoned from some netherworld. Its claws dug deep into the ground, wrenching up dirt and leaving thick gouges in the surface as it slithered up from the depths. This was no horse.

It was foolish to ride the drake-like monster he reserved for battles and war only to hunt down a girl in her desperate bid for freedom. His beast would find it a pathetic excuse for exercise. He would have to have him fed well to compensate. Perhaps tonight the girl Evie would learn what it meant to be eaten by a dragon.

Slinging himself onto the back of the creature, he kicked his heels into its sides. It let out a roar.

The hunt was on.

SIXTEEN

What was it like, to die?

What was it like, the moment it came?

Honestly, Aon could not remember. Very much like the moment of drifting off to sleep, it came upon him slowly. When he would lay down in his crypt and let himself slide away, he could never pinpoint the moment it arrived.

But coming *out* of death was another matter entirely. It was not an experience that anyone outside of those claimed by Under were ever graced with. And it was for very good reason. The act of returning from the other side of death and into life... was painful.

Oftentimes more so than the act that put him there.

Although, to be fair, it had been many—*many*—hundreds of years since anyone had ever killed him. He only experienced it when he was forced to sleep in his crypt and let that idiot Edu rule in his stead. But such was the cost of his foolish war, and he paid it without complain.

Very well. Without much complaint, he corrected himself. He was wont to do that frequently; talk to himself within his mind as if there were more than one of him sharing the space. Perhaps there was. It was hard to tell, some days.

He sat up from his crypt. Forcing himself out of his slumber too quickly was an agonizing ordeal. It was a little secret of his, that he kept a thread-line to the waking world should he need it. Far be it from him to trust the giant moron to care for the world while he slumbered. No, he always maintained a secret way out of his forced sleep should he need it. He had not yet found the need to wield such a thing.

But for this girl? This mystery, this charmingly naïve mortal rejected from the Pool, as yet as she went in?

For her, he would rise early. Regardless of the liquid iron that it sent burning through his veins. Pressing his hands into the lip of his sarcophagus, he tipped his head down and found that he could not fill his lungs with air. They would not obey. They were deflated—or perhaps too full—to move.

Silence.

His heart was not beating.

Well, that was irritating.

Ah. So, this would be why they rose over long periods of time. Why it might take years for one of them to become conscious. Now he had confirmation on his theory of what might happen to him should he force the matter, as he just had.

Fascinating. This is miserable. He would have laughed, could he inform his body that it needed to move. To live. To breathe. To not be so unflinchingly *cold.* He was a corpse, after all, now struggling to return.

He did not have time for this.

More aptly, she did not have time for this.

Edu was going to kill the girl. He knew it, as certain as he knew the moons would rise. Edu would see her as a threat, and Navaa had confirmed it. To keep her "dark secrets" from his grasp, the girl's brains would be dashed out upon the stones. He could only hope he had not taken too long enough as it was.

Finally, his lungs obeyed, and he pulled in a long gasp of air. *Oh, that was heaven.* The hot iron in his veins receded, if just a little. Enough that he could shift. To try and stand. To try and climb out of his sarcophagus.

Damn his heart, it was still not moving. He balled his right hand into a fist and slammed it into his chest, attempting to start it. Once, twice, and on the third impact, he felt it lurch. Heard the thrum that had been so noticeable in its absence.

Fascinating how the sound of one's heartbeat is only understood by its absence. Observations for another day. He climbed over the edge of the stone, one leg at a time, and stood. Nearly falling to the floor in a heap, he kept himself standing with a hard grasp of his metal claw on the edge of the stone.

Silently, he shouted at his errant limbs. Screamed at them to obey him. By sheer force of will alone, he straightened up and tugged his suitcoat straight, and combed a hand through his hair. He would be presentable when he arrived.

First impressions are key. For while they had met before in dreams, this waking world was a far cry removed from the muddied and illusive world of visions. He was... excited... to meet this girl. Aon was not frequently anything of the sort. That anticipation matched his will, two horses tethered together to a carriage and both together pulled his unsteady and entirely unready body to action.

He did not even bother to return home. He doubted there was time to do such a thing. For in his great lengths of years, for all his eternity that stretched on long beyond the point that it should, there was one odd fact that remained perfectly clear to him. When fate wished to change the world, it did so very quickly. His life may drag on for a hundred years without incident; but when the compass of the world changed, it did so in a matter of moments.

And so, he knew, the girl's life hung in the breadth of seconds.

But how to find her? He knew where Edu's keep was, of course, so that gave him some sense of guidance. Some narrowing in of the field. Lydia had found her way into his dreams, and he into hers, on several occasions. They had a bond; a strange link he did not understand. But he would use it to his every advantage.

Summoning the strength, he bent the shape of the world on its axis and stepped between the folds. It was bending space at a point like folding pieces of paper—simply thinking about the world in a different way. Space was relative, after all.

At the same moment, he reached out to the girl. Sought her mind through the maddening multitude. He called upon the same power that granted him the ability to speak into the minds of his servants; to Navaa and the others. Once he had touched a mind—or in her case, hers had touched his—he could tug upon the string like that of a puppet.

There you are, my darling.

* * *

Suddenly those horseback riding classes Lydia could have taken as a child seemed less silly than they had at the time. Maybe she should have done that instead of the piano lessons, after all.

At least the bug-horse had plenty of jagged bits to hold onto, with its exoskeleton and all. She did everything she could to cling for dear life. A road curled into the woods ahead of them, and while she had no clue where she was going, it was the only path she could see.

She kicked the thing to move faster, and it was happy to oblige. It was in a full gallop now, which was actually far more comfortable than all the gear shifts it took to get up to that speed. For the moment, she felt free. The wind whipping her hair behind her felt amazing. It was cold, and she might care about having no sleeves if she weren't being driven forward on adrenaline alone.

The woods around her were pitch-black and terrifying. It looked like every nightmare forest from a fairytale, twisted and warped with bare branches and jagged vines. There was no doubt in her mind that monsters lurked in the darkness.

The wind and the speed and the sheer overwhelming need to hold on consumed her thoughts. Lydia barely heard a roar from back toward the keep. Barely listened to the echo of creatures in the woods. It didn't matter. Right now, she had one task—forward. Ahead. Away. Freedom.

Maybe she could make it to the city Yej on horseback. Maybe she could make it to the gate in the center of town and back home to Earth. Without a mark on her, maybe she could get away and not be found again. She had a lot of maybes.

There were two moons in the sky that had risen to replace the turquoise one. One was a deep and saturated magenta, and the other was a rich blue. Where the two mixed, it almost looked like white light, like a typical moon. But the shadows were strange and one color or the other, alternating depending on the angle.

The horse seemed overjoyed to race down the road, seeing an empty stretch ahead of them, tossing its head as it galloped along. They both wanted freedom for different reasons, but for now, they had the same goal.

It was funny how quickly things could change. It was incredible how quickly things could happen.

Chaos wasn't predictable. All it took for everything to change was a split second, and there was no going back. Only after the moment was over could you parse it out and figure out exactly what happened when, and in what order, to try and lay out a timeline and better understand it. Like a car crash.

She had been racing through a nightmare forest on a nightmare horse in a nightmare world. Hope had bloomed in her heart for the first time since this whole mess had begun.

Then she was on the ground. Everything hurt. Her body ached with searing pain as if she had been in a car accident. The wind had been knocked out of her, and for the second time in as many days, she couldn't breathe. Her head was bleary, her sight clouded.

Finally managing to pull a gasp into tortured lungs, she felt the clarity the cold air gave her.

Lightning.

There had been a flash of lightning. It had come down on the path in front of her, the air splitting with the tangy taste of electrons and ozone. Blinding and deafening, the sound still left her ears ringing.

The lightning had struck the path in front of her and her horse, sending the creature hauling up to a stop and rearing on its back legs. It had thrown her to the ground in the process.

That was why everything hurt. At least she hadn't landed on any rocks. Small favors.

After she had managed to catch her breath, she pushed herself up off the ground. She was trembling, her hands were shaking. She felt loosely connected to the world around her. But she had to get back on that damned creature and keep going. There was no way the lightning strike hadn't been on purpose. It was far too convenient.

It took every ounce of strength she had to push through the searing pain and back up to standing. By the sharp sting and the sticky feeling on her leg, her knee was bleeding. With a shaking hand, she pushed her hair away from her face.

When she looked up, all her thoughts of freedom were dashed away. All hope was gone.

Edu hadn't been the source of the lightning bolt.

A figure stood there watching her, standing at the spot where the blast had struck. He was tall and thin, the carefully tailored suit belying the lithe muscle underneath. Dressed entirely in a mix of black fabrics and cast in stark contrasts by the glow of the overhead moons, he was imposing.

When he spoke, his voice was just as it was in her dreams. A knife, wrapped in velvet—a low tenor that was as dangerous and dusky as it was sharp.

"Hello, my dear."

Aon.

* * *

What were you trying to do, little one?

It wasn't until now that it struck Aon as interesting that he had not appeared inside a jailcell. He had not been summoned to her side in the depths of Edu's keep. Instead, he was in the woods. And that girl had been atop a creature, making a bid for the horizon. A bid for escape.

How wonderful!

A little resourceful thing she must be, to gather the ability to escape from someone who was as intractable as Edu. He built his home as he built his ego; stubborn, brute-force, and unrefined. And yet, there she was, lying on the ground. Pushing herself up to her feet.

His heart soared for her. That she had the strength of will to fight back. The simple question remained; would she do the same with him? Certainly, she had expressed her dislike for his methods and his madness in dreams. But now that her life was on the line in far more finality than before. For here, he could *truly* hurt her.

Although he may not need to. She was injured. That much was plain to see as she wavered on her feet. She pushed her hair away from her face and lifted her head. She saw him where he stood in the center of the path, and he knew he cut an imposing sight.

He would have it no other way.

"Hello, my dear."

What will you do now? Will you turn and run? Will you scream or beg for mercy? Will you pay me in tears for your safety?

He watched. He stood, some twenty feet away as he was, and waited. He let her decide what path they may now yet travel together. It seemed like the "polite" thing to do—she had chided him on his manners, after all—and he was also endlessly curious.

Sometimes, it was more interesting to see the vermin play within their maze; to eke out their own directions. Most often, he felt like the mastermind of the maze, watching those beneath him scurry about and struggle to find their way through the darkness, when he could see the whole.

But this one was not vermin. This one was not so weak. He watched as something flashed over her face. Hope, followed by hopelessness, followed by resignation, followed by... dignity. No; not dignity. *Defiance.*

This one was certainly not vermin.

How he *wanted* her.

She raised her head to look at him, did her best to straighten her shoulders, and tried, as far as he could tell, to fashion a façade of bravery on her stunning features.

You think to stand your ground? You think you are so stalwart? We shall see, precious thing. He could not help but laugh. A low chuckle that carried forebodingly through the darkness of the trees. He took one step toward her, then another, slowly—carefully—letting her change her mind. Giving her fear a chance to simmer and rise to a boil. Would she bolt?

Tucking his human hand behind his back, he closed the distance between them.

Still, she has not moved. Still, she has not run. His heart was pounding in his chest, fully awake now from his forced death. It was not the adrenaline of a return to life that sent such adrenaline through his veins. It was *her.*

No one holds their ground against me. No one does not dare shrink away. Not even the Priest holds the line when he is pressed.

Oh, but how she was trembling. She was nearly quaking; in fear, in injury, in many things. But she did not retreat from him. She did not stand down. She held her shoulders and her head high, and though her eyes had now focused upon his tie and not the visage of his metal mask, she stood firm.

Good girl. Impressive. But I know how to scare you. I know how to call your bluff. He raised his metal gauntlet to her face and held the claws over her skin such as they caught the moonlight. She flinched but... did not retreat.

He let out a quiet noise despite himself. The sight of the instrument of her recent torment in her sleep should have sent her stumbling away from him in terror. But she did no such thing. A flinch of fear, of waiting for him to tear her face off from her skull, but otherwise, she stayed still.

His heart may have skipped a beat, but he was not certain.

Curling his claws in toward his palm, he let the backs of his metal knuckles slowly brush down her cheek. He had intended to run the tips of his metal fingers there instead; but something inspired him to be more gentle with her. She had held her ground against him. He could pay her some kindness in return.

Something flashed over her features. No, in fact, a myriad of things ran through her in succession. He watched her struggle with something internally, playing things out in her mind and trying to find a way forward. She did not want to cave into his embrace such as he might dream, but neither did she run in fear or sink to her knees in surrender.

"Tell me, what was it I have just witnessed play out upon these lovely features of yours?" He kept his voice low and soft, not wanting to startle her. He had to know.

She shot him an incredulous glance as if he had asked her to explain if the moon was made of cheese. She had not expected him to speak, perhaps. At least not with such a line of reasoning.

He wished to snatch her in his arms. Drag her to his home, kicking and screaming. He wished to tear her clothes from her body, to rend them from her with his bare hands. She stood before him now, trembling and skin freckled in goosebumps. He would have her naked beneath him in such a state for a very different reason. He would have her cry as she wept for him to take her—and to take mercy upon her—in the same breath.

Shoving the thoughts back into the corner of his mind from whence they had escaped, he scolded himself. Control was key, before something *else* rose to overtake his restraint. But his voice, when it left him, was a low and deadly rumble, nonetheless. "Indulge me..."

Lydia was left stammering. She could sense the tiger that loomed in the shadows, even if she could not see it for what it was. She was no idiot. They had a few minutes to themselves, and he let her take the time to summon her wits enough to speak.

She took a breath, and finally found her words. "Crying won't help. Begging won't work. I can't run, and struggling will do more harm than good. I... I've lost. The only thing left to do is die with pride." Her hands clenched at her sides as she spoke, and then went limp as she spoke of death.

She accepts her fate. She knows she cannot escape me. She tried to run from Edu—tried to escape him—but can sense that I am the far more dangerous one.

It did not do anything to help him suppress his ravenous hunger for her.

"*Mmh*, beautiful." Aon stepped in closer, ignoring how she went rigid in response. Using the talons of his gauntleted hand, he stroked through her hair slowly, brushing her waves away from her face and tucking the strands behind her ear.

She pulled in a breath and held it. Her eyes went wide, and she froze. She knew that even if he were being gentle now, that may change in short order at any moment.

He smiled, though she could not see it. "Then you are no fool, my clever thing, to see the truth so easily. Good. That will make this far more interesting."

"If you're going to kill me, please do it already." She was positively quivering in fear.

Kill you? Killing you is the last thing upon my mind. Not until we have had a chance to truly become acquainted. He curled his metal fingers under her chin and broke her gaze from where she had fixated on his tie pin. "Oh, my dear. Kill you? Why ever would I do that?" He knew the answer to the question quite keenly. He had given her every reason to fear him. But he wished to dismiss the concern aloud; and to do so and yet maintain his position of power in the conversation, he would have to have her admit her worry. He always preferred to offer the counterargument. Never the leading charge.

She looked at him in perfect disbelief. She, too, could not believe he did not understand. "I mean, last time... you..."

And so, they waltzed. "Ah. Yes." He shifted his weight from one foot to the other, his masked face turning away for a moment. He pretended to look thoughtful. "I think perhaps I have given you the wrong impression. What I did was merely to teach you a lesson. Hopefully, I will not have cause to demonstrate another."

What I have done to you in dreams was done to show you what pain may come. I am not interested in playing that particular game with you; for as you are mortal, it would be disappointingly brief. Squishing a gnat is not a sport. I take no joy in killing a fly. But we may play other games yet, my dear. You are still a mystery; and I do hunger for a real puzzle to solve.

Turning back to her, he pressed the point of the thumb of his clawed hand against the line of her lower lip. Stepping in closer, he hovered just a few inches away. "No, beautiful darling, you are the first unusual thing to happen in this forsaken world in a long, long time. I have no desire to kill you. Far from it."

"I..." She suddenly looked woozy. She blinked as if drugged.

Oh.

Yes.

Right.

She was a mortal.

Her eyes seemed to turn glassy, and she wobbled.

He had forgotten—*he had entirely dismissed*—that she was hurt. That the fall from her horse had not healed nearly instantaneously as it would have for any of them.

Her hands grasped his arms suddenly. She reached out to hold on to anything that was nearby that could keep her upright. And at the time, that was... him. Letting out a low hum in his throat, and finding that he enjoyed her hands clinging to him entirely far too pleasurable, he wrapped an arm around her waist, and pulled her up against his body.

She is so warm. So soft. So wonderfully alive. The reality of her was so much better than the dream. Her heart was pounding in her veins, her face was flushed, she leaned against him, even as she fought against the surrender. But her body was betraying her. It was hurt, and he was a port in a storm.

"Well, now, all you had to do was ask." Far be it from him to resist the temptation to tease her.

"I... don't feel so good." She slumped against him. The poor girl was hurt and hurt quite badly.

"My poor little thing. It is quite all right. You are injured. Do not fight it. I will take care of you."

"Edu's going to kill me." Her words were growing more slurred.

Aon was barely listening. She smelled of summer and a

strange tinge of chemicals. He wanted to press her against him and never let her go. "Do tell."

"To keep me away..." Her head reeled to one side. Lydia clearly couldn't hold onto consciousness anymore. Her grip on it was slipping, just as her hands were falling from clinging onto his coat.

No, my pet. Edu will not touch you. He will never lay a hand on you again—even if you were to beg for it. You are in my care now. And I do not think I wish to let you go. "He will not harm you. With me, you will be safe. I promise."

Her eyes rolled into her head before the lids slipped shut. She was unconscious. He picked her up into his arms, holding her like one might a—

He struck the thought dead where it stood. He would not give it credence. Her head rested against his shoulder. Victory made his heart soar. She was alive. Edu had been bested. He had reached her in time.

And now?

She was *his*.

A LETTER FROM KATHRYN

Dear reader,

I want to say a huge thank you for choosing to read *King of Flames* If you did enjoy it, and want to keep up to date with all my latest releases, just sign up at the following link. Your email address will never be shared and you can unsubscribe at any time.

www.secondskybooks.com/kathryn-ann-kingsley

I hope you loved *King of Flames* and if you did I would be very grateful if you could write a review. I'd love to hear what you think, and it makes such a difference helping new readers to discover one of my books for the first time.

I love hearing from my readers – you can get in touch through social media or my website.

Thanks,

Kathryn Ann Kingsley

www.kathrynkingsley.com

x.com/vodriel

instagram.com/kathrynannkingsley

PUBLISHING TEAM

Turning a manuscript into a book requires the efforts of many people. The publishing team at Bookouture would like to acknowledge everyone who contributed to this publication.

Commercial
Lauren Morrissette
Hannah Richmond
Imogen Allport

Cover design
BRoseDesignz

Data and analysis
Mark Alder
Mohamed Bussuri

Editorial
Jack Renninson
Melissa Tran

Proofreader
Catherine Lenderi

Marketing
Alex Crow

Melanie Price
Occy Carr
Cíara Rosney
Martyna Młynarska

Operations and distribution
Marina Valles
Stephanie Straub

Production
Hannah Snetsinger
Mandy Kullar
Jen Shannon
Ria Clare

Publicity
Kim Nash
Noelle Holten
Jess Readett
Sarah Hardy

Rights and contracts
Peta Nightingale
Richard King
Saidah Graham

Printed in Great Britain
by Amazon

53832502R00135